MAGGIE COBBETT

ANYONE FOR MURDER?

HAD WE BUT
WORLD ENOUGH

SWINGS AND
ROUNDABOUTS

OMNIBUS EDITION

To Jan
with very best wishes
from Maggie

Published by GuyRichardson

CONTENTS

ANYONE FOR MURDER?

ANYONE FOR MURDER?
TOO MUCH BLOOD ON THE AXMINSTER
THE HIGH PRICE OF A SMILE
MURDER IN THE SECOND ACT
EYE OF NEWT AND TOE OF FROG
A HELPING HAND
NOTHING ON HER CONSCIENCE

HAD WE BUT WORLD ENOUGH

PLENTY MORE WHERE SHE CAME FROM
CUBAN NIGHTS AND YORKSHIRE MORNINGS
GRANDFATHER'S DREAM
A DEAL'S A DEAL, ISN'T IT?
FINE FOR A FLING
YOU CAN ALWAYS TELL A YORKSHIREMAN
FIRST CHRISTMAS

SWINGS AND ROUNDABOUTS

BURP
FINGS AIN'T WHAT THEY USED TO BE
KARMA
THE FAT RASCAL
VAINGLORY

CONTENTS

SWINGS AND ROUNDABOUTS (CONT)

NOT QUITE NESSIE

NEMESIS

AN UNEQUAL STRUGGLE

MONEY WELL SPENT

CRABTREE MANOR

HE WHO LAUGHS LAST

FOR MORE STORIES, VISIT
WWW.MAGGIECOBBETT.CO.UK

Anyone For Murder?

Anyone For Murder?

"Go on, Julie," said Sergeant Metcalf. "You might even enjoy yourself. Or are you too grand now to help out an old friend?"

Julie Carr flushed and looked round the canteen to see who might share Rosemary Metcalf's opinion of her. Julie's transfer to CID had met with general approval at the station, but she knew that it still inspired envy in some quarters.

"Of course not," she said. "I'm just not sure what the higher ups would make of it."

"You mean the Super?" Julie bit hard on her scone. No trainee detective constable would willingly incur his wrath.

"He wouldn't know," insisted Rosemary. "You don't suppose he watches that rubbish, do you? Anyway, your name wouldn't be in the credits and chances are that your face wouldn't be seen clearly either." Julie's fiancé Ian caught the last few words as he put his tray down between them. Still in uniform himself, he was both proud and protective of his wife to be.

"What's Rosemary trying to rope you into this time?"

"Something that's right up Julie's street, Ian."

Julie spluttered through a mouthful of crumbs, "Just because I've done a bit of am-dram? It's hardly the same thing." She had rashly sold tickets to her colleagues for a performance of *An Inspector Calls* and could still see the row of grinning upturned faces when she fluffed her lines.

"No. It's much easier than that. It's not a speaking part and there'll be no need to ask about your motivation for the role either."

"Very funny! Anyway, Ian and I have plans for tomorrow. It's not often that we both get a day off in the middle of the week."

"What plans? Slogging around the sales looking for the best deals in coordinated tableware?" Rosemary saw from their expressions that she was not far off the mark and pressed on. "You'd be doing me a big favour, honestly. I signed up before I realised that it was the kids' sports day and they'll be so disappointed if no one turns up to cheer them on. With Neil working away and both sets of grandparents on holiday, well, you can see what it's like. I'd do the same for you in a crisis. You know I would."

"Oh, all right." Julie knew when she was beaten.

Hardly a crisis, Julie thought glumly, as a sharp wind pierced her thin outfit. It seemed strange to be back in uniform, especially since the one she was wearing was baggy and dated back to the time when the regulation skirt and handbag suggested that policewomen were generally kept out of harm's way. Of course, the costume had been ordered to fit Rosemary's more generous proportions. With a large mortgage and the demands of a growing family, it was small wonder that she seized every legal means that came her way to make extra money. Extra money, indeed! How apt! Rosemary had been first in the queue to respond to a call for local extras for an episode of *Anyone for Murder?* It was ironic that she had been cast as a policewoman. And now here was Julie, up since first light and standing in for Rosemary for a half share of the fee. Oh well, she could add it to the honeymoon fund.

She only had a vague idea about the plot. Grumpy amateur sleuth Miles Spangler, played by veteran Shakespearean actor Seaton Fortescue, was about to stumble upon yet another recently dispatched murder victim. He would then make the local police look like complete idiots and solve the crime in forty-five minutes flat of prime television time. Cast and crew regularly left their studios in London for locations up and down the UK. For this episode, they had taken over part of the Knavesmire to be as close as possible to York Racecourse. Miles Spangler, disguised in a similar deerstalker and cape to those worn by racing pundit John McCririck, was going to investigate a case of horse nobbling, the grand dénouement to take place at a gala dinner in the Gimcrack Suite.

Seaton Fortescue had not waited for filming to start before getting into character. Complaint followed complaint. His breakfast had been cold by the time the runner brought it to his trailer, parked in splendid isolation at the far end of the unit base. The make-up girl had made him look like a clown. His already well polished brown Brogues needed to be cleaned again. He demanded last minute alterations to the script.

"That's why Lisa dried just now," observed the camera man next to Julie, patiently waiting for the next take. "And now look at the poor girl!" The leading lady was in floods of tears and having to be comforted by the director.

"That's just typical of *Mister* Fortescue," he continued. "Don't ever make the mistake of using his first name. He's had people fired for less. Thinks television is beneath him." He struck a dramatic pose. "Not quite the RSC, dontcha know, old chap!"

"I expect he makes a lot more money doing this," ventured Julie.

"You bet, but he's never satisfied. I could tell you a few things about the way he's treated people that would make your hair curl." As the camera man raged on, Julie stifled a yawn and listened politely. The novelty of being on set had worn off and it helped to pass the time.

During the tea break, Seaton Fortescue rudely refused to sign autographs for some elderly fans hovering at a respectful distance. They turned away, disappointed, and their places were taken by two teenagers in zippered hoodies. One of them propped his bicycle up against a tree and threw back his hood to reveal a black beanie hat with a brightly coloured badge pinned onto the side at a rakish angle. He fished into his pocket for his camera phone and pointed it towards the star. The sudden roar made half the crew spill their drinks and the director drop his keys. Julie was closest and obligingly retrieved them for him. Seaton Fortescue was in full flow.

"Take photographs of me, you young whippersnapper, and I'll sue!" The boy's response was colourful. Someone sniggered and the actor's haughty features contorted with anger.

"You there!" he bellowed. "Get rid of these louts!"

"Me?" asked Julie, taken aback.

"Yes, you, WPC Plod. They won't know the difference. Go on, woman. Jump to it!"

More amused than irritated, Julie walked across and said with a calm air of authority, "Come on, lads. Do us all a favour."

Beanie Hat hesitated. "I only wanted a photo for my Gran. She watches every episode."

"Oh, come on," said his friend. "It's a rotten programme anyway." They cycled off together, but Beanie Hat, once at a safe distance, turned round and stood up on his pedals.

"I'll get you for this, you pompous old..." The director buried his head in his hands as Seaton Fortescue erupted again.

Breaking for lunch came as a relief after a morning spent mostly standing around waiting for something to happen. Julie had only been used twice, once to push an old bicycle across the set and the second time to run back blowing her whistle. She was hungry, but the pecking order decreed that extras were served last and all the tables in the dining bus were occupied by the time she climbed on board with her food. As she looked round for somewhere to sit, a friendly voice said:

"You can squeeze in here with us, if you like." Julie smiled gratefully at the runner who had been in trouble earlier for serving Seaton Fortescue a cold breakfast. The actor was under discussion again and it seemed that everyone at the table had good cause to loathe him. Julie was fascinated.

"If he's such a pain, why doesn't the director give him the boot?" Her own superiors would never tolerate such behaviour.

"From what I've heard, it's not as simple as that," replied the make-up girl next to her.

"And that's not all," chimed in the props man who had issued Julie with her bicycle and whistle, "although I shouldn't really be telling you this." By the time lunch was over, Julie felt that she knew everything there was to know about Seaton Fortescue, up to and including his hat size.

The man under discussion failed to turn up for the first scene of the afternoon and did not respond to the runner's nervous tap on the door of his trailer.

"Perhaps he's having a power nap," called out one of the assistant directors. "Try again, harder this time, and then stand well back." There was no response to the second knock either.

"He's got Radio 3 on full blast," reported the runner.

"Well try the door." She did.

"It's locked."

The director sighed. "I suppose I'd better go over there myself. He's probably sulking about something." Everyone watched as he crossed the site and knocked politely, then banged on the door with his fist.

"Mr Fortescue? Are you all right in there?" Finally, he took out his keys. Moments later he was back, ashen faced and trembling. "Someone call an ambulance, quickly. And get the police!" Julie reached for her warrant card. Ordering everyone else to stay back and taking care not to disturb anything, she peered in through the door. There was blood everywhere. At the fold down table, Seaton Fortescue was slumped over the remains of his lunch, the wooden handle of a steak knife protruding from the side of his neck. On the seat by the broken window behind him was a little metal badge with a distinctive red, blue and white crest.

"More youth knife crime about to hit the headlines," sighed Detective Inspector Ackroyd. "Looks like an open and shut case. Hoodies strike again!"

"Why do you say that, Sir?"

"Well, look at this, Detective Constable." He held up the carefully bagged badge. "It obviously belongs to the youth who threatened the victim earlier."

"What makes you so sure that it's his, Sir?"

"Take a closer look. I don't have to tell you what it is, do I?"

"No, Sir. Of course not. York City Football Club. I'm a supporter myself." The DI looked at her thoughtfully and she hastened to add, "Whoah, Sir. It's not mine, if that's what you were thinking."

"Never crossed my mind, Carr. There are some fibres attached to it, no doubt from the lad's hat. Shouldn't be hard to match. Now then, by your own account the two of them looked too young to have left school, so we'll ask the local head teachers to find out who was missing this morning – with or without permission. My guess is that we'll find the answer at York High School. It's an easy cycle ride from here and it's a sports college, so they'll all be keen on football. Julie sighed. DI Ackroyd's love of an open and shut case was legendary. No wonder that he had risen no further.

"With respect, Sir, I don't think you should jump to conclusions just yet. There's another York supporter you might care to question."

The following morning in the canteen, Rosemary Metcalf had a rueful look on her face as she limped to the table.

"What made you think that it might be the director?"

"Evidence gathered from crew gossip," replied Julie, trying hard not to look smug. "It's not just that everyone hated the victim, but the ratings for the show were going down too. The director wanted to kill off Miles Spangler and give Lisa the lead in a spin off series. He couldn't, because Seaton Fortescue had a water-tight contract and friends in high places. I think he knew a bit too much about the director's private life as well. Anyway, he was desperate and that fracas was just the opportunity he'd been waiting for."

Rosemary was puzzled. "But how did he get hold of that boy's badge?"

"He didn't. It was his own. I noticed when I picked up his keys that they were on a YCFC key ring. The director's a local lad, apparently, although he moved down to London years ago."

"You clever girl to notice that! I won't pretend I'm not jealous," she added, "But you were doing me a big favour."

"It turned out to be mutual," grinned Julie. "I even got a pat on the back from the Super. Now then, tell me more about winning the mothers' race. I suppose twisting your ankle like that was payback for twisting my arm, but at least we both have something to celebrate."

Too Much Blood On The Axminster

She was not snobbish or house-proud, but too much blood on the Axminster was more than she could take. Enough was enough. She had lost track of the number of times he had forgotten to bring an essential piece of equipment, been called away to a 'family emergency' or failed to turn up at all. Her attempt that morning to cajole him with homemade cake and a mug of tea had been a big mistake. He had kicked off his shoes and taken root in a comfortable armchair, from which he was holding forth about the finer points of his trade in preference to getting on with the job in hand.

"Underlay, you see, is the key to it all," he droned. "Then you need a sharp knife, of course, and a tucker and a knee kicker."

"A what?"

"One of these. It's for stretching the carpet over the gripper." The tool he held out to her was solid looking with teeth at one end and a heavily padded butt at the other. Rather like him, she thought, as his mobile phone rang and another hasty departure beckoned.

"Sorry, I've got to... Ouch!" He had stepped straight onto the length of carpet gripper waiting to be fitted. Blood spurted out of each nail hole as he hobbled towards the door across the only section of Axminster that he had fitted so far.

"I'll have to go for a tetanus jab."

"You're going nowhere, Colin, until you've sorted out this mess and finished the work I'm paying you for!"

He laughed. "Try and stop me, lady."

She did. Later on, his remains would join those of Brian, the bungling builder, Doug, the drunken decorator and Graham, the gormless gardener. First, though, she had to tackle the stain and then search the Yellow Pages for another fitter.

The High Price Of A Smile

The police investigation was well underway by the time I arrived at the Station Hotel. A white tent had been erected in front of the main door and scene of crime officers were swarming in and out. Part of the car park had been taped off and a uniformed constable was doing his best to hold back a growing crowd of onlookers.

"I'm sorry, Sir," he was saying to Peter Mosby, a reporter from the local rag. "You and your photographer can't go through. No one's allowed. I've got my orders." Mosby and I had met before, when he was covering a court case I was involved in. As an expert witness, of course. I wouldn't want you to get the wrong idea about me.

"What's going on, Mr Mosby," I asked. It took him a while to place me, then he smiled.

"Oh, hello again, Mr Wolfson. It looks as though someone's called time on one of the barmaids. Foreign girl, I think. The one with the nice smile. Pretty. Well, she was before this happened. She was first in this morning to get ready for opening time and it looks as though she disturbed a burglar. When the landlord got here, he found her sprawling behind the bar. Quite a mess, I gather."

I knew at once which barmaid he meant. As he babbled on, my mind drifted back to my first encounter with Agnieszka. She'd caught my eye as soon as I walked into the bar. It was a busy evening and I had to wait a few minutes for her to serve me, but watching her at work was no hardship. I pretended not to hear the other barmaid asking me what I was drinking.

Agnieszka stood before me at last, eyebrows raised in polite enquiry. A half of bitter was all I usually ordered, but I didn't want to look hard up.

"I'll have a double Scotch, please. And one for yourself, sweetheart." That deserved some flirtatious banter, but she didn't even smile or thank me. Far from it. She took my order silently, her lips clamped together like my wife's fingers on the purse strings.

The man next to me at the bar muttered, "You won't get anywhere with Smiler, pal. Do you know why the regulars call her that? It's because she's as miserable as that old git in *Last of the Summer Wine.*"

"But she's beautiful! What can she possibly be miserable about?"

"Oh, aye, she's a real Page 3 girl. Figure to die for. Every bloke's fantasy. Until she opens her mouth, that is."

"Bad language?"

He laughed. "No, that's not what I meant. I don't suppose she'd know how to swear in English, anyway. She hasn't been over here long enough. Her choppers are the problem."

"Choppers?"

"Her gnashers. Her pearly whites. Except that they're not. They're gruesome. I asked the landlord once why she didn't do something about them and he said that she wouldn't spend the money. Apparently she's supporting her whole family back home."

My professional curiosity wasn't the only part of me to be aroused and I ordered drink after drink and handed over larger and larger tips, using up in one evening the pocket money my wife allowed me for the month. Each time Agnieszka put a glass down in front of me, I tried in vain to strike up a conversation with her. In the end, I had to play the customer from hell to make her speak. Accusing her of bringing me the wrong drink didn't work. It was only when I threatened to tell the landlord that she'd short changed me that Agnieszka gave in and opened her mouth.

"Please, no. No tell boss. I sure I give you right money." In all my long career, I'd never seen worse teeth. They were all over the place, like the stones in a Victorian graveyard. Actually, that was putting it mildly. Not only that, some of them were missing or broken and the rest were rotten. I patted Agnieszka's hand and told her that it was all right. My mistake. Then I wrote a few words on the back of one of my business cards and passed it over the bar.

The next evening, we agreed on her new dental plan. I'd take care of her needs if she'd take care of mine. My wife had never been very forthcoming in that department and I'd learnt not to push it. So, it wasn't long before Agnieszka and I both had plenty to smile about. Business and pleasure mingled happily in my surgery while my wife was visiting her mother, an ordeal I only escaped under the pretext of doing the practice accounts. We were very discreet. On the odd occasion that I called into the Station Hotel, Agnieszka paid no more attention to me than to any of the other customers. Her rapidly improving smile was the talk of the bar and she had quite a fan club. What a shame that some little toe rag who'd broken in to steal a few bottles of spirits or rob the cigarette machine had put paid to her high hopes for the future.

The DCI spotted me waiting by the police cordon and called out to the constable to let me through.

"Nasty business this, Mr Wolfson. You've helped us on tricky cases in the past and there are some strange features to this one. Not the sort of thing we'd expect from your common or garden villain caught in the act. This looks personal. Hate crime. A jealous boyfriend, maybe. The landlord tells me that the victim had a lot of admirers. Ambitious too. She'd just signed on with a glamour agency. We'll be liaising with the police in her home town, of course. There might even be a gangland connection. You'd better put on one of these suits, Sir, and we've got some gloves for you."

Agnieszka had put up quite a struggle to save herself. You can't be squeamish in my job, but I did find the sight distressing. It wasn't the blood or the lacerated hands that upset me. It was realising with horror who had done this and why. The killer had gone for Agnieszka's jugular with a dental chisel and then brutally undone all my careful work. Bits of veneer and broken porcelain crowns lay all over the floor behind the bar. I sighed. A pair of thin rubber gloves from the clinical waste bin at my surgery had been discarded nearby and would have more than enough of my DNA inside to send me down for life.

The killer's gloves had left the scene with her. I don't know how my wife found out about Agnieszka and me, but I'm sure of one thing. Cosmetic dentistry doesn't come cheap and it was the expense, not the infidelity, that Mrs Wolfson was going to make me pay for.

Murder In The Second Act

"A murder mystery weekend!" exploded PC Dandy McLean. "Talk about a busman's holiday! It's the last time I buy a raffle ticket."

PC Terry Taylor snatched the brochure. "It's got a lot more going for it than tracking down Colonel Mustard in the library with a dagger," he leered. "Look at this! A cosy retreat with a crackling fire in every bedroom." Dandy brightened up and his fiancée, Leona, was thrilled.

"Shall we have to dress up?" she asked.

"Probably," replied Dandy. "It says here that we'll get details in advance of our characters and a general outline of the set-up. There'll be some professional actors too, working to a rough script."

"I hope you're not squeamish, Leona," joked Taylor. "They guarantee at least one corpse for you to examine."

"Social workers can't afford to be squeamish, Terry!" she fired back. The brochure included quite a few gory photographs, but Leona wasn't going to be put off. She wanted a chance to prove that her powers of observation were as good as Dandy's.

A few weeks later, they were on their way to The Old Manse Hotel. It was a long drive from Edinburgh and they were amongst the last to arrive. A buzz of conversation drew them into the bar, where people dressed in 1950s style clothing were nervously sipping their pre-dinner drinks and trying to weigh each other up.

"Here we go," hissed Dandy, as a blonde bombshell in bright pink chiffon bore down on him. Her silver-haired companion gazed appreciatively at Leona, whose usual off-duty jeans and jumper had given way to an emerald-green cocktail dress from Oxfam.

The blonde pouted, saying, "Aren't you going to introduce us, Tony?"

"Of course, Gloria, my dear," he replied in an accent several notches higher up the social scale. "I'm afraid my memory isn't quite what it was, but I'd like you to meet young... "

Dandy caught on quickly. "Tim, Uncle Anthony, and this is my intended, Emily. Lord Driscoll, darling," he added, stepping back to allow Leona and Tony to shake hands.

"How do you do, my Lord."

"Delighted my dear."

"Well," said Dandy a few minutes later, as they took their places for dinner. "No prizes for guessing who the pros are."

"I've seen him in one of the soaps and her face looks familiar too," agreed Leona.

Before the first course was served, the hotel manager urged his guests to remain in character throughout their stay and to react spontaneously to each situation presented to them. Dandy's neighbour started the ball rolling.

"I never thought that my brother would take up with one of those dreadful Good Time Girls you read about in the newspapers," she hissed.

Her stage whisper reached Gloria, who chortled, "Nothing wrong with having a good time, dearie. You look as though you could do with one. Where's that husband of yours? Has he traded you in for a younger model?"

Nice one, thought Leona. Across the table from her, a dark-haired man peered at Gloria through thick spectacles and listened intently as the conversation warmed up, the women taking the lead.

"Not our sort at all." said one.

"Gold digger," sniffed another.

Lord Driscoll ignored the comments for a while, then rapped on his wine glass and announced proudly that he and Gloria were engaged.

Gloria broke the stunned silence by crowing, "Me and Tony's going to get hitched, so deal with it! There'll be no more scrounging off him neither, not with the big family we're planning."

His Lordship coughed. "I say, steady on, old girl."

"Why?" she snapped. "They need to know. You've already changed your will, haven't you?"

"Well..."

She ignored his hesitation. "Then they won't get another penny from you, dead or alive!"

Whether or not the will in question had actually been changed, it became increasingly clear as the evening went on that Gloria's plans must be foiled. Dandy/Tim and Leona/Emily wanted to buy a farm in Canada. Uncle Crispin was next in line for the title and the estate. Aunt Lydia had been promised the Dowager Lady Driscoll's jewellery, including the diamond solitaire now on Gloria's finger. Lady Patricia could not afford to divorce a faithless husband and short-sighted Cousin Frank needed to pay off a blackmailer. Nephew Tarquin had gambling debts and twin nieces, Camilla and Drusilla, were hoping to start their own fashion label. Suspects all, but who was the first victim going to be?

Dandy and Leona were just going down to breakfast the next morning when the scream that everyone had been waiting for rang out.

Dandy smiled. "That's it. My uncle's a goner."

"Or Gloria, perhaps," suggested Leona.

The hotel manager was the picture of concern. "The chambermaid has just found Lord Driscoll dead in his bath. I'll phone the police. In the meantime, no one must touch the scene of the crime."

"What makes you so sure that it was a crime?" asked Cousin Frank.

"Just a hunch, Sir."

As soon as he left, everyone rushed upstairs. Gloria sobbed ostentatiously as they crowded in to view the body. The bath had been drained. Only the small towel preserving Lord Driscoll's modesty and the occasional twitch of a nostril betrayed that he was playing a part. Aunt Lydia seized the pink hairdryer lying next to him.

"Look, that's what has killed our dear Anthony," she gasped.

"It might have been an accident," ventured Leona.

"Don't be ridiculous," snapped Uncle Crispin. "Anthony was in the Guards. Do you honestly think he'd own a thing like that?"

"Murder by electrocution!" said Lady Patricia triumphantly.

"It's been proved that dropping a hairdryer into a bath is very unlikely to kill anyone," argued Dandy. "The fuse would blow as soon as it hit the water. I remember a case..." He stopped in mid-flow as Leona trod hard on his foot.

As Cousin Frank leaned over to take a closer look, his heavy spectacles fell into the bath. Leona picked them up to hand back to him and their eyes met for a moment before he rammed the spectacles hastily back onto his nose.

"Thank you, young lady."

As the morning progressed, fingers were pointed at almost everyone. Any of the women, including Gloria, might have owned a pink hairdryer. On the other hand, a man could have used it to put the police off the scent.

Gloria was magnificent, weeping noisily in between targeting one member of the family after another. When she finally withdrew, Uncle Crispin summed up what the others had been wondering.

"Why would such a good actress waste her time on this nonsense?"

"Maybe she can't get anything else," suggested Dandy.

"You're right there, young Tim," agreed Cousin Frank.

Leona looked thoughtful. "I can tell you why she's been reduced to this. I didn't recognise her at first with the blond wig, but I saw her once at the Palace Theatre in Manchester. Then she was given a part in the West End and got herself into trouble for upstaging Anita Fitzgerald on the opening night. Anita went to pieces and her understudy had to go on. That's not the worst of it, though. Anita ran out of the theatre in tears and was knocked down by a taxi."

"I remember that," said Camilla. "She wasn't killed, but she lost the baby she was carrying. Her husband had Gloria – it's her real name, by the way – blacklisted."

"How could he do that?" asked Lady Patricia.

"Because Nicholas Fitzgerald is one of the most influential men in British theatre and with a temper to match his red hair."

"Odd looking chap, though, when you see a close up," remarked Uncle Crispin idly. "He's got heterochromia."

"Hetero what?"

"Heterochromia. Underneath that floppy fringe of his, he's got one brown eye and one blue."

Dandy was curious. "How on earth do you know that?"

"From an article in the free magazine at my optician's. There were photographs of several celebrities with the same condition."

Drusilla had followed Gloria out and came back laughing. "Talk about shattering the illusion," she sniggered. "I've just seen his late Lordship being waved off in a taxi. They might at least have ordered a hearse!"

"Well, that's that," said Tarquin. "The end of Act One, I should think."

Numbers were boosted after lunch by the arrival of two policemen and the family solicitor, who let slip that Lord Driscoll had had second thoughts about changing the will in Gloria's favour.

"That must explain what the row was about," cut in the manager. "I heard them at it last night while everyone else was still downstairs."

Confronted with this incriminating evidence, Gloria denied vigorously that there had ever been any argument between her and her fiancé. "And don't think that you're going to frame me neither!" she shouted, as she stormed out of the lounge.

"Far too obvious," whispered Dandy to Leona. "Whoever the murderer is, it won't be Gloria."

There was a lull during the afternoon. As soon as the policemen had taken brief statements from everyone and departed, the guests were free to explore the surrounding countryside for a few hours. Dandy and Leona were glad to have some time on their own at last.

Gloria failed to put in an appearance at dinner. As there was still no sign of her after the meal was over, a search began. Uncle Crispin, Aunt Lydia, Cousin Frank and Tarquin offered to comb the hotel, while the others went out into the grounds. Inside a little gazebo at the furthest point from the main building, they found the actress lying on her back in a pool of blood.

"What a fantastic make-up job!" breathed Leona. "Doesn't it look real, Dandy? Sorry, I mean Tim."

"Far too real, I'm afraid," was the grim reply. "Keep back, everyone!"

"Who put you in charge?" demanded Drusilla, trying to push past him to get a better view of the body.

"I'm Police Constable Dandy McLean, Madam, and I'm putting myself in charge, until the local force gets here."

"For real?"

"Of course not," said her twin. "It's just part of the plot."

Dandy glared at both of them. "Can't you see that you're looking at a real murder here? This woman's been shot."

"Go on," scoffed Tarquin. "That's Kensington Gore she's covered in."

"What?"

"Theatre slang for fake blood." It took Dandy's production of his warrant card to make them take him seriously. He herded everyone back to the hotel lounge and ordered the manager to ring for the police.

"It can't have been any of us," protested Aunt Lydia. "We'd only just met the poor woman. I want to go home." Dandy's large frame was blocking the doorway.

"No one's going anywhere just yet," he said firmly.

Tugging at his arm, Leona whispered urgently, "Before the local police arrive, there's something you should know about the man calling himself Cousin Frank. When he dropped his specs into the bath..."

"So, another crime solved, young Dandy," said Sergeant Brian Patterson, back at the station in Edinburgh.

"Mostly down to Leona this time," admitted Dandy. "She'd noticed Cousin Frank's odd eyes and realised who he was. His hair was dyed, of course. He'd stage-managed the whole thing. Written the script. Hired Gloria through a third party."

"But surely he'd ruined her career already. Wasn't that enough?"

"No. He wanted his wife to make a comeback, but Anita Fitzgerald hadn't got the guts and was using Gloria as an excuse. You know the kind of thing – 'I'll never step onto another stage while that woman's still alive!'

Well, now she might, but Nicholas Fitzgerald won't be in the audience for a very long time."

Eye Of Newt And Toe Of Frog

"You not going to that concert on Saturday," I say. "Papa and I forbid."

"But Mama," she try again, "All my money gone on the ticket to see Goldie Shone live... and my new autograph book." Rita wave a little red leather book under my nose. It have her name on it in gold letters.

"Very nice," I say. "Room for everyone at church to write their names."

"People at church!" Rita look at me as if I slap her face. "Not them! I only want important people's autographs. Famous people like Goldie Shone."

"What the matter with you, child?" I say back to her. "Those people no better than us. Look, you want names in your book, you ask your Papa and me. Ask your Auntie Comfort. Ask the Reverend Nathaniel Odinga."

"It not the same, Mama," Rita argue. "You and Papa good people. Auntie Comfort and Reverend Nathaniel Odinga good too but not... celebrities."

"What you mean, celebrities? Singers like your Goldie Shone?" I ask her. "And that Eminem you used to like so much? If I his Mama, I wash his mouth out with soap. Such ugly words he sing."

"Not only singers," Rita say. "Oh, you know, Mama." She think for a moment. "Footballers too, like David Beckham. Everyone want to meet him."

"David Beckham! When he not chasing a ball round a field, he show-ing off what should be kept for his wife. On posters. All over London. I no bat an eyelid if I meet a man like that."

"Oh, Mama, you so old fashioned," Rita carry on, squeezing my hand and sighing as if that normal and I the one out of step. "How about a film star like Tom Cruise?"

"How many wives he had?" I ask.

"Only three so far, Mama," she tell me now. And she with her Mama and Papa bound together in holy wedlock twenty-seven years by father of the Reverend Nathaniel Odinga.

"What makes them so special, these... celebrities?" I ask her.

Rita's eyes shine. "Oh, Mama, it the way they live, the clothes they wear, the places they visit, the people they know."

"You think you inferior?" I ask her. "You don't live so bad since we come to this place. You have clothes. Decent clothes. Clothes that cover what should be covered. Clothes that don't give boys bad thoughts. You visit places. Nice places. You know people. Good, God fearing people. You inferior to no one, daughter. You bright. Pretty. Take a look in mirror."

"I know, Mama, but it not the same," she say. "I not look the way they do. Have my hair and nails done every day and buy *designer* clothes. Goldie Shone never wear the same suit twice and he fly his own helicopter to gigs."

That quite enough. I send Rita up to her room. It seem that only money talk in this new country she love so much. The money that the Reverend Nathaniel Odinga call the root of all evil for those that set too much store by it. Not like back home, where our people poor but have respect. My Rita not going to any concerts to meet her... celebrities. Papa and I say no. She cry. She scream. Make no difference. She stay here. Do homework. Is better for her. Not like girls I see in street with yellow hair and painted faces and skimpy dresses that not hide their shame.

Next morning, our Rita gone. Clothes too and her little red leather book. She join other fools who follow false idols. Autographs just the start, the Reverend Nathaniel Odinga tell Papa and me. We sick when he tell us about fallen girls he call *groupies*.

Papa so worried he go to arena on Saturday, find this naughty girl we love so much. He got no ticket for concert and must wait at gates. Maybe he drag Rita home by hair when she come out. Maybe he even take belt to her bare skin, like he never do before. Better that than she offer it up in sin to Goldie Shone for an autograph in her red leather book. Papa wait for hours, then thousands come out together and he no find our girl. Maybe she see him and hide, or maybe she catch the eye of Goldie Shone already and heading for the fiery pit. Papa come home alone and weep. Then he grab chest. Bad pain. Then he gone. We taking him home to bury when our Rita found. That good man deserve warm sun on his bones."

The desk sergeant sighed. He felt sorry for the dejected little woman in the neat felt hat, but so many youngsters went missing in London every year. Just past her sixteenth birthday, Rita was too old to be a priority and he forgot all about her until after the murder.

Goldie Shone's biographer was later to state that Rita's rise from obscurity to celebrity girlfriend had not been an easy one. Exchanging the comforts of home for a live-in job at a drab hotel in Bayswater, she worked long hours for less than the minimum wage. Every penny she could spare went on tickets, mainly to see Goldie Shone. She was nowhere near the front of the crowd of autograph hunters at the first concert. At the next, a bouncer went off with a large pile of books and returned with a scrawled signature in each. Rita might have been content with that, if she had not compared notes with some other fans and discovered that several different hands had been at work. There was nothing for it but to hand her book to Goldie Shone personally. By the fourth or fifth concert, she had learnt from the more experienced girls how to wheedle a backstage pass. Reeling from one sweaty embrace to another, Rita looked a mess the first time she got near to the star. He completely ignored her nervous request and stalked off with a triumphant blonde on his arm.

It took bleaching her hair and crashing a birthday party for one of the roadies for Rita to get Goldie Shone's attention. His trademark gold teeth flashing, he wrote a dedication in her little red leather book and moved in for the kill. After so much pallid flesh, he told his hangers-on, he was ready to taste some darker meat. According to him, Rita's last thought before she leapt willingly into the fiery pit was of the Reverend Nathaniel Odinga. It made her laugh, but maybe that had more to do with the intoxicants supplied during the evening than her pleasure at defying all that he stood for.

Being the much envied blonde of the moment, wined, dined and showered with expensive gifts, was fun for a while, until Goldie Shone tired of his new toy. Desperate to hang on to her irresistibly handsome but dissolute and ill tempered celebrity boyfriend, Rita tolerated the verbal abuse and beatings he doled out to her during his drug-fuelled tantrums. Even when a photograph of her badly swollen face appeared on the front page of all the tabloids, she refused to press charges. The use of marijuana, heroin and crack cocaine became the focus of *her* life too and it was not long before she and Goldie Shone disappeared into rehab together. He emerged first, clowning for the camera and with a new blonde on his arm. Rita, pregnant and abandoned, tried to kill herself and lost her baby instead.

Goldie Shone shrugged his shoulders, unaware at that point that his own days were numbered. Following newspaper reports of the suicide attempt and miscarriage, he was taken ill on his own doorstep. Just after signing an autograph for an unidentified blonde, seen by a passer by only from the back, the singer lost all use of his limbs and fell into a coma from which he never came round. The cause of death, according to the official report, was a strong poison of unknown origin, probably administered through the skin. Someone present at the autopsy leaked to the Press for an undisclosed sum that it was 'real eye of newt and toe of frog stuff.'

The police interviewed Rita and as many of her predecessors as they could locate, but each and every discarded blonde had a solid alibi. Other lines of enquiry were pursued. A crazed fan? A stalker? A professional rival? A jealous husband in drag? That the identity of the killer remains a mystery has helped to make Goldie Shone's biographer a very rich man.

"You ready to go to the cemetery, Mama?"

"It hot today. I just need to put on my hat."

"That old straw thing?"

"Papa like this hat. He buy it for me after I make offering to Loa Damballah and you born. Maybe the Reverend Nathaniel Odinga feel moved to buy nice hat for you when we get back."

"Maybe you right, but first we visit Papa. Look, Nathaniel's father give me these wild lilies to plant around his headstone."

"Nathaniel? You ahead of yourself, girl! You not Mrs Nathaniel Odinga yet."

"But you already decide, Mama. Nathaniel think it his idea, he so happy bring me back to grace. We fine, as long as he never know the truth about Goldie Shone."

"That wicked man curse himself when he hurt my baby and my baby's baby. You got the trowel?"

"Of course, Mama. You got the wig?"

"Here the nasty thing! We bury it deep, girl. No more call for blondes in this family."

A Helping Hand

I found Marcus standing near the edge of the cliff, his bicycle thrown down carelessly behind him on the grass. He was so intent on the waves crashing against the rocks hundreds of feet below that he didn't hear my approach and nearly jumped out of his skin when I called out his name.

"Oh, it's you." He relaxed for a moment but still looked as though he had all the cares of the world on his thin shoulders. "Don't come any closer, or..."

"I'm not going to stop you jumping, you know, if that's what you really want." That surprised him. Maybe he had been expecting a rugby tackle. In any case, he gave me a very wary look and took a step even closer to the edge.

"What else can I do? I've got myself into such a mess." I didn't deny it.

"I thought of going into hiding," he continued in a shaky voice, "but Stephenson has contacts all over town and he'd track me down sooner or later." He paused, waiting for me to tell him that he was exaggerating. I didn't and he started to babble.

"You know what they'd do to me then, Stephenson and his boys?" I nodded and waited for him to continue.

"I was only the go-fer, but I saw enough that night to send them down for life."

Another pause, then he looked me straight in the eye and said, "You're going to tell me to go to the police, aren't you?" I shook my head.

"What would be the point of that? Stephenson *owns* the police around here." He looked thoughtful, though, and when he spoke again his voice was a little firmer. "Maybe if I could get far enough away, I could turn Queen's evidence. Isn't that what they call it?" I nodded again.

"In exchange for protection and a new identity." There was a gleam of hope in his eyes. With no help from me, he'd chosen not to end his life. Maybe I could teach those Samaritans a thing or two about technique.

In the meantime, I had my own job to do. It only took one push to send him flying over the edge.

Nothing On Her Conscience

Miss Eleanor Pettigrew's long white neck was perfectly set off by the dark chestnut curls that floated around it and came to rest on her slim shoulders. At thirty-seven, her appearance was striking enough to make people wonder why she had chosen to work in a provincial library in preference to pursuing a career in the media. Indeed, her looks were such that it came as a surprise to new acquaintances that she was still single, although she was vague enough on the point to make them realise that this was not a subject to pursue. What a waste, they generally concluded.

At this particular hour, on this particular day, considerations of marriage or celebrity were far from Miss Pettigrew's thoughts. Indeed, the only things that came to mind as she gasped her last breath were the dark band pressing tightly into her throat and the quiet words of malice from the person determined to end her life.

Miss Pettigrew's body slid to the cold marble floor and quiet footsteps indicated that her killer was leaving the building. Everything else was silent. The library had been locked for the night and no one alive remained inside.

Mildred Baker had the unhappy distinction of being the first person on the scene the following morning. As head cleaner, she was one of the few people entrusted with keys to the rambling Victorian building. Protecting its fabric, especially its black Belgian marble staircases, had long been her mission in life. She would have made the staff and visitors change into slippers on arrival if she could. Nothing was more injurious to marble than grit, not even the stiletto heels of the young library assistants. At least, *they* only spilled their coffee onto the cheap carpet in the staff room. Visitors, positively encouraged to buy drinks from the machines on each landing, slopped them all over the place and added insult to injury by upending their polystyrene cups over the ornate brass finials of the banisters.

Miss Pettigrew had always been kind to Mildred and was the only person who seemed remotely interested in the rival merits of different cleaning products. "You're right, Mrs Baker. Marble may be a stone, but it's porous and it stains easily. Are the floors here sealed? If not, you'll certainly have to tackle any spills straight away, even if it does mean inconveniencing the public. I'll see if Mr Warburton can arrange to get some heavy duty mats for the entrance too, to catch some of that grit." Mildred almost wept to find a kindred spirit and had treated Miss Pettigrew with doglike devotion ever since.

"As beautiful as Lorraine Chase, she is!" she told her grandson Sam, toiling away at his homework on their kitchen table. "But better spoken. And watch you don't spill your Coke on them books I took out for you."

Miss Pettigrew's crumpled body lay at the bottom of the main staircase. In death, she was no longer beautiful. Above the bruised throat, her face was purple and bloated, contorted with pain. Her tongue was protruding; her eyes, wide open, bulged. The whites had turned pink where tiny blood vessels had burst. Mildred almost missed the pearl choker dangling from one of the finials. She picked it up and put it into her overall pocket.

"Just for safe keeping," she said later on, as she handed it over to the police. "Miss Pettigrew wore it for work every day."

Detective Chief Inspector Trelawney sighed. "You do realise, Madam, that nothing should be touched at a crime scene, let alone taken away? How can the SOCOs be expected to do their job otherwise? It's bad enough that there's no sign of whatever the killer used to strangle the poor woman."

Mildred bristled. "Well, don't look at me for that! Anyway, how was I supposed to know that you were going to close the library down for the day? Any Tom, Dick or Harry could have picked up poor Miss Pettigrew's pearls and then you'd never have seen them again."

Derek Warburton, Group Librarian, agreed. The library attracted all kinds of riff-raff these days, from feral children who came in to mock the readers to the malodorous old woman who spent her days snoring in the reference section. Political correctness and social inclusion policies were two of the many things making him count the days to his retirement.

"I wish I could show them the door, Chief Inspector, and that's the truth." Secretly, he would have like to do the same to Miss Pettigrew's many admirers, men of all ages who plagued her with spurious enquiries. She always did her best to help, unless they became over familiar and tiresome. Her green eyes could turn in an instant from a warm and sympathetic regard to a withering glance, but it never seemed to put them off. On the contrary, their devotion increased and she was never short of invitations to expensive dinners or the theatre, all of which she refused.

None of these things was ever on offer to Iris Smalley, Assistant Librarian (Information and Local History), who returned home every evening to a drab house and querulous elderly mother. She was deeply envious of Miss Pettigrew's ability to attract, yet keep at arm's length, every male who came into her orbit, including Mr Warburton. Poor besotted man. He was almost old enough to be Miss Pettigrew's father and yet had had such a hopeful look on his face when he invited her to a gala evening at the Film Society. When she gently turned him down, his eager smile had fallen to the marble floor and shattered. Miss Smalley would never forget the hurt in his eyes.

"It was only yesterday and in front of me, Chief Inspector. He was completely humiliated. She said that she had a prior engagement every evening for the next few weeks, but he didn't believe her."

"Is Mr Warburton in the habit of inviting out colleagues? Yourself, for example?"

She flushed. "Certainly not. But then I don't dye my hair or plaster myself with make-up like some women my age."

"Miss Smalley would like to go out with him, though," said the next interviewee. Debbie Clark was not one to mince her words. "She's had her eye on Mr Warburton ever since his wife died and I think she'd have worn him down by now if Miss Pettigrew hadn't come along. 'Edith bloody Swan-neck' she called her yesterday and said that she'd like to wring it for her." Horrified by what she had blurted out, she added, "Not that she meant it literally, of course, but she must have been upset. I've never heard her swear before."

"And when did Miss Pettigrew start working here?"

"I'm not sure exactly. About six months or so, I suppose. It's all in her personnel file and Mr Warburton would know."

"And how did she get on with the female staff? Was she close to anyone in particular?"

"She was friendly enough, I suppose, but she didn't have much in common with the older ones, her not being married. They talk about their children all the time or what to get their husbands for dinner."

"And the younger ladies? Yourself, for instance?"

"Well, she came out with us once or twice when she first started here, but it didn't really work out."

"Why was that?"

"Well, she didn't fit in. She wouldn't tell us anything about herself. At her age, she must have been round the block a few times, but she wasn't letting on. She was a bit prim too."

"In what way?"

"In the way she dressed, for one thing. Smart, of course, but very buttoned up. That's all right in the library, of course, but even when we went clubbing she kept her scarf on."

"What sort of scarf?"

"Oh, one of those posh ones they sell on aeroplanes. Hermès or something. She said that she'd caught a cold on holiday and her throat was still rather sore. I mean, in a club you want to wear a little top and show off your assets, don't you?"

Trelawney coughed. "Not personally, Miss Clark, but I take your point."

"Not that it stopped the men lining up to ask her to dance."

"And did she?"

"No, and neither did the rest of us. They just walked off when *she* turned them down. It was a complete wash out."

"So Miss Pettigrew had no friends on the staff?"

Debbie snorted. "Well, not unless you count Mildred. She thought Lorraine Chase was the bee's knees until she met Miss Pettigrew."

Not knowing whom to notify about the death when the emergency number on Eleanor Pettigrew's personnel file was not recognised, the police had to break into her neat flat to look for clues to her next of kin and other contacts. There were none, but some correspondence from Thailand strengthened Trelawney's suspicion that Miss Pettigrew might not be quite what she seemed; unlike Edith Swan-Neck, King Harold's faithful mistress. He had the Internet to thank for that last piece of information.

There were no messages on the answering machine and the last call received by Miss Pettigrew turned out to be from a public telephone box late the previous night. Trelawney told a constable to take the letters, a photograph album and a school exercise book found in the flat back to his office at the police station. They would keep until he had the autopsy report and it was time to round up the suspects. With no sign of a forced entry at the library, there would not be too many of those.

Sam Baker, another fan of the Internet, happily handed in his homework assignment on time. Unwanted by either of his parents, his examination prospects had looked bleak when he first came to live with his grandmother. Then she had found the extra support he needed in the shape – and a very nice shape too – of the new lady at the library. Gran had been quite frank with him.

"I'm no good to you, Sam," she had said. "You know I can't make head or tail of your school work myself. I certainly can't afford to buy you a computer either, so I hope you'll be sensible and appreciate what Miss Pettigrew has offered to do for you. She's willing to give up her evenings for as long as it takes to get you through your exams. You needn't worry about the school finding out that you're having extra lessons. She's promised not to tell anyone and she's not charging us either, so no worries there."

"No one ever does anything for nothing, Gran. There must be something in it for her."

Sam had been truculent ever since his parents' divorce had landed him on Mildred's doorstep. Being forced to change schools halfway through his GCSE courses had damaged his confidence and the low marks he was getting had done nothing for his self esteem. To his grandmother's relief, though, the awkward schoolboy blossomed under Eleanor Pettigrew's tuition and *she* seemed to get a lot of satisfaction from his progress. He soon developed a crush, of course, but Mildred was confident that he would be let down gently. After all, sturdy and handsome as he was, he was less than half Miss Pettigrew's age.

The computer problem was solved when Miss Pettigrew said that Sam could come round to the library on the evenings when she had to work late. Mildred went with him the first couple of times and sat in a corner with her knitting while he surfed the Net for the information he needed, but after that she was glad to have the house to herself for a couple of hours. With Lorraine Chase no longer in *Emmerdale*, she turned to *Coronation Street*.

Mr Warburton was the first person to be interviewed again after the autopsy. Horrified by the photographs Trelawney laid before him, he struggled to speak.

"Of course I had no idea," he said at last. "No one here did. What do you think I am, Chief Inspector? Do you really think that I'd have suggested a... date, if I'd known? Yes, of course I was disappointed to be turned down, but now... Can you imagine the scandal if we'd been seen out together and then all this had come out? It would have been all over the tabloids!"

His protestations seemed genuine enough, thought Trelawney, dismissing him and calling in Miss Smalley.

She sniffed disdainfully. "Well, I always thought looks like that were too good to be true, but I could never have imagined anything like this. Never in a million years! It's disgraceful. And to think how we were all taken in, even dear Mr Warburton. He must be devastated."

Debbie Clark took a broader view. "Well, what a nerve! We were all convinced. And all those men lining up! To be fair, though, I suppose

Miss Pettigrew... it's hard not to say that, even now I know... never gave them any encouragement."

The photograph album remained closed when Trelawney had Sam Baker seated in front of him. The boy was trembling with emotion and close to tears.

"Tell me about your tutoring sessions with Miss Pettigrew, Sam, especially the ones that took place when you were by yourselves in the library."

"What do you want to know? She just let me use one of the computers. She taught me more about ICT than I ever learnt at school and it was great for other subjects too, especially Biology. I've never been good at that and she helped me a lot."

Trelawney hesitated. "Sam, did Miss Pettigrew ever say or do anything to make you feel uncomfortable?"

"You mean because I didn't always catch on quickly to what she was trying to teach me? No, she was always very patient and encouraging."

"That's not what I meant. Did she ever get too close. Physically, I mean. Try to touch you inappropriately?"

Sam stared at him for a moment and then shrugged his shoulders. "I should be so lucky!"

"Well, did any of your conversations turn to sexual matters?"

"Only for school. As a matter of fact, the course work I've just handed in was about gender issues. How some people feel that they've been born into the wrong bodies and even have surgery to put it right. Like Hayley in *Coronation Street*, you know."

"And how did Miss Pettigrew feel about that?"

"She said that everyone should be more understanding and she was right. I'd never really thought about it before. It's not their fault and people shouldn't turn against them when they want to change. Gran won't talk about things like that, but Eleanor didn't mind."

"You called her Eleanor?"

"When we were on our own. Gran wouldn't have thought it was respectful. She always called her Miss Pettigrew, what with her being a librarian and Gran only a cleaner."

"And Mrs Baker knew nothing about this conversation?"

"Not unless she's been going through my notes. I found out a lot more about it on the Internet."

"Such as what?"

"Such as men who would rather be women having their Adam's apples reduced to make them less obvious. Oh, and having their vocal chords tightened."

"Why would they do that?"

"To give themselves higher voices, of course."

"And you wrote all this down?"

"Yes. I'm hoping to get an 'A' out of it."

Trelawney sat back and closed his notebook. "Thank you, Sam. I don't think I'll need to speak to you again for the time being."

Mildred Baker's first reaction to the photographs of Eleanor Pettigrew's former life was one of revulsion.

"Disgraceful!" she hissed.

"Do you think people like that deserve all they get, Mrs Baker?"

Startled by the question, she looked up sharply. "Now I never said that, Chief Inspector, but I do feel very let down."

"Is there anything you wish to add to your earlier statement, now that you've had time to think about it?"

"I don't think so, thank you."

Despite careful searches of the library itself, the surrounding area and the homes of the various suspects, the murder weapon was never found. As the police pursued their enquiries, they discounted the library staff one by one and switched their focus to the victim's past. The media had a field day when it came to light that Eleanor, who had begun life as Edward Pettigrew, had earned money in any way she could to finance her visits to an exclusive private clinic in Bangkok. Reporters desperate for lurid details tracked down former employers, lovers and clients, but none had links with the area or could be proved to have been anywhere near at the time of the murder.

Mildred Baker watched with satisfaction as Sam, now resplendent in a Sixth form tie, received his prize for an outstanding performance at GCSE. Six months had gone by since a few bits of library gossip and her own observations had started to make her wonder about Miss Pettigrew. Although still desperately hoping to be proved wrong, she had made the phone call that lured her idol back to the library after hours and challenged her to remove the pearl choker. The sight of the neat scar convinced her that the person she had admired and trusted was grooming Sam for her own twisted purposes. Deaf to her victim's protestations of innocence, rage gave his grandmother the strength to put him beyond any possibility of corruption. Mildred would go to her grave convinced that she had done the right thing.

The spare drive belt from the library's vacuum cleaner went straight back into her little cupboard on the first floor landing, with nothing to show that it had ever taken a human life.

Had We But World Enough

Plenty More Where She Came From

Mary stared in despair at the pile of dirty dishes. Out of all the work she had to do, washing up was what she hated most. The water from the hot tap had run cold long ago and Madam would be angry if any of her girls complained of being given a greasy plate. Did she dare to venture out of the kitchen and ask permission to switch on the water heater for a few minutes? No. Mary must keep out of sight. Madam had made it very clear that visitors to the house must never see the little ghost who cleaned the bedrooms, scrubbed the toilet, served the meals and did everyone's laundry.

At home, there hadn't been many dishes to wash, even in the good times. Water was carried up from the river by the women and girls, gossiping and laughing as they balanced the bright plastic bowls on their heads and prepared to trudge uphill in the midday sun. They dreamed of a pump of their own, but no foreign aid reached their village, even when the river ran dry and the maize shrivelled in the little plots. That was the year that Mary's mother died and left her father to cope helplessly with his eleven children.

Mary longed to see them all again before their faces, already fading from her memory, disappeared altogether. She sighed and reached for the kettle. She would have to wash the dishes a few at a time and hope that they were all dried and put away before Madam came to check up on her. She must never forget that she was the lucky one. It had to be true. Her father had said so. Her older brothers and sisters had said so. Auntie Doris had said so. Madam often said so. Even Madam's girls said so sometimes, on nights when business was brisk and they wished they could lie down alone for an hour on Mary's little camp bed in the store room.

How long had it been since her father's second cousin, Auntie Doris Netabango, came to the village and offered to be her guardian? Mary's father had taken a lot of persuading to let her go, but how could he deny his third daughter the opportunity for a better future? Her sisters, as curious as she was about city life, had pleaded to go too, but Kesia and Promise were needed at home. Mary was the lucky one. Auntie Doris would see that she worked hard and went to school. Later on, when she entered a profession, she'd be able to send money home to help her family. A week later, Mary was on her way.

So far she had learnt only to do as she was told and keep her mouth shut. Her first ever ride in a bus was fun, but Mary hated the crowded and chaotic entrance hall of the little airport. There, Auntie Doris introduced her to Uncle Adolphus and disappeared, but not before Mary noticed some grubby notes changing hands. Uncle Adolphus took her on the plane to a much larger airport and handed her over to Auntie Grace, who gave her a smart new outfit to wear and said that she was taking her to England. Homesick already, Mary started to cry. Auntie Grace told her in front of the other passengers to be a brave girl and go into the Ladies with her to wash her face. As soon as the door closed behind them, she gave Mary a hard slap and threatened more if she didn't cheer up at once. She was eleven years old, not a baby, she scolded. Should Auntie Grace send Uncle Adolphus and Auntie Doris a message to tell Mary's father that his unselfishness was being thrown back in his face? How would he receive back such an ungrateful daughter? Mary knew the answer to that one. Like her brothers and sisters, she was no stranger to the cane her father used to punish disrespect. All the village parents agreed that childhood beatings were the way to instil good nature for the future. Mary wiped her eyes with the back of her hand, choked back her tears and smiled bravely as they rejoined the other passengers. Once through the departure gate, there was no turning back.

Exhausted and emotionally drained, Mary slept through most of the long flight. A man in uniform scrutinised the papers Auntie Grace handed him, while Mary looked at her sandalled feet and said nothing. The ride in a big black taxi through streets of tall buildings and well dressed people was exciting and Mary had her nose pressed up against the window all the way. Then they came to an area where the buildings were not as tall and the people were not as well dressed. A couple of white men lounging on the pavement stared curiously at Mary as Auntie Grace took her to a shabby door with an iron grille in front of it and rang the bell. Madam opened the door and led Mary inside. When Mary looked back over her shoulder, Auntie Grace was getting into the taxi.

"I'll show you where you're going to sleep," Madam said. "And then you can make a start on the washing up. We've been waiting for you."

Two years had gone by and there had been a lot of washing up. Madam had most of the food sent in, but she wouldn't allow her girls to eat with their fingers from the cartons. Why should they, when Mary was there to clear up after them, and anyway it would ruin their long painted nails. Occasionally, Madam ordered fresh meat and vegetables and stood over Mary while she prepared them and stirred the pot.

Sometimes she lashed out at Mary with the hot ladle for letting the food stick to the pot or adding too much chilli pepper. None of the other girls raised a hand to help her. They were all frightened of Madam too, even the favourites who were allowed out occasionally, accompanied by Zef or Liridon.

The twins' casual brutality kept all the girls in line. Big swaggering blond men in their thirties, they could do no wrong as far as Madam, their mother, was concerned. There were generally five or six girls living in her house, the line up changing at Madam's whim or just to offer the regular gentlemen variety. Some girls stayed for several months and others only for a few weeks. Some cried when they were brought to Madam's house. Others cried when they were moved on. Most had picked up some English, but few spoke it well. It didn't matter. The gentlemen didn't come round for conversation.

Mary wore the same ragged overall and broken sandals every day and smelled of cooking fat or disinfectant. Madam supplied the other girls with skimpy underwear and shiny shoes with high spiked heels to wear on duty. The rest of the time, they sat around bored in their grubby dressing gowns, smoking and watching television programmes they couldn't understand. Some wore thick make-up to hide their bad skin and even thicker make-up when they had bruises or cigarette burns to conceal. They had to douse themselves with perfume when gentlemen were expected. At first, Mary thought that those who came regularly were suitors. She remembered girls in her village primping and preening for their future husbands and wondered if her older sisters had received any proposals yet. Maybe Mary would surprise them one day by arriving home married to a rich Englishman! It had taken a sad eyed girl called Vicki Chang to put her straight.

"I don't know when I'm going to leave here, but my Auntie Doris told me that if I work hard I'll be trained for a profession," Mary confided shyly one morning when she was collecting Vicki's discarded underwear to wash.

"Darling, the only profession you're going to be trained for is ours. You're just lucky that Madam doesn't think you're ready yet and finds you more useful in the kitchen." Mary's dreams of a bright future had crumbled that day, but what could she do? She had no idea where she was, much less how to let her father know that he had been deceived.

Now, as she washed the last few dishes and started to dry them, she thought with a shudder of how Madam had said that she was filling out nicely. Her periods had started at last, a source of shame and embarrassment to her but, it seemed, one of satisfaction to Madam.

Even worse, Zef had begun to take a different kind of interest in her, Zef who had always been quite kind. He had even sat her on his knee sometimes and read her a story in his broken English. Lately, though, he'd started to look at her strangely and had slid his hand between the buttons of her overall, his hard fingers probing and squeezing. He laughed when she squealed and let her wriggle away. Liridon was watching and the next day he caught her round the waist when she was working and pressed himself up against her. Mary knew that there would be no point in appealing to Madam, however much it hurt when the twins began her training.

At least, she consoled herself, it meant that someone else would be brought in to take over the washing up. As Madam often said, there were plenty more girls where she came from.

Cuban Nights
And Yorkshire Mornings

I choke on spikes as I look at the phone bill. Calls to the same number in Cuba have accounted for most of it and his family has no telephone. I sigh. Most tourists bring back cigars or Che Guevara T-shirts, but trust me to go one better and come home to Leeds with Carlos Estrada in tow.

It all started with a song. *Yo no se mañana* was playing the evening that I took my first tentative steps on the scuffed wooden floor of a wine bar off the Headrow. Salsa classes had started up there and my friend had dragged me along. It did not take us long to realise that we were in the wrong place. Women outnumbered men by at least three to two.

"Sorry," mouthed Suzanne. "We'll just have a drink and go, shall we?" I almost agreed, but the music was catchy and we had already paid at the door, so we stayed. By the end of the evening, I was hooked. Suzanne never went again, but I became a regular. A skilful system of rotation ensured that no one was without a partner for long and much the same applied to the social breaks in between classes of different levels.

"Remember this, girls," Ricardo and Alina warned newcomers, "It's just as acceptable for you to ask the guys as for them to ask you." It was. Like the 'girls', the men were of all ages, sizes, shapes and backgrounds, but nothing mattered except their ability to lead and ours to follow. It was not long before salsa had completely taken over my previously bleak social life.

With my new friends, I ventured into local clubs and soon found myself dancing three or four nights a week. When the opportunity arose to sign up for an organised salsa holiday in Cuba, I shut up shop and off I went.

The flight from a grey and weepy Manchester was a long one, but the atmosphere on board the plane was exuberant and crackling with expectation. We landed on a hot, sunny afternoon and even the long queue to have documents scrutinised by unsmiling officials could not dampen our spirits. Neither could the battered concrete buildings, the smoke from fleets of rusty old American cars or the packs of stray dogs we passed on the way to our hotel. Our escort, Lola, indicated a few examples of restoration work going on.

"But Havana has a long way to go to catch up with Miami," she added sadly.

"Is it true that more Cubans live in Miami than in Havana?" piped up an enquiring voice.

"No, but Miami is now home to many exiles. My brother, for example, followed his dream and now runs a bar on South Beach with his American wife."

My own dream of dancing in one of the heartlands of salsa was about to become reality. Having unpacked, showered and swallowed a couple of mojitos in the little bar, I was ready for anything.

In order to correct the gender imbalance, the holiday organisers had recruited some English speaking local men, smartly dressed in tight black trousers and pristine white shirts, to join us and it was not long before I was singled out by Carlos for special attention. The intimate hold and need for constant eye contact had been drilled into me from my first lesson, but these he took to a new level. His combination of a playful approach, startlingly good looks and the ability to float us both effortlessly through

the most complicated manoeuvres had me entranced. Soon he was escort-
ing me back to the hotel, mouthing sweet nothings into my ear and yes,
of course, I was flattered. Lola might as well have been talking to a brick
wall when she took me aside to advise caution.

"You know that Carlos is... only after one thing," she began hesitantly.
I cut her short.

"A good time? Well, so am I. Isn't that why we all came to Cuba? To
enjoy ourselves and learn some new moves?"

"That's not what I meant..." she called out to my retreating back.
Maybe Lola, who wore no wedding ring, was just jealous, I told myself.
Even in a country full of handsome men of all shades, who could fail to
be dazzled by Carlos with his charm, his black hair, smooth olive skin
and neatly trimmed moustache?

Looking back on it, I can see that the warning signals were there almost
from the start. Carlos never took me to his home, but members of his
extended family would turn up uninvited – by me, anyway – almost every
time we sat down for a meal and take little persuasion (his) to join us. He
demurred politely the first time I offered to pay the bill, but then it became
routine. The night we went to see Los Van Van, Cuba's most famous salsa
band, we were accompanied by a cousin and his girlfriend who seemed
to take it entirely for granted that I would be buying the tickets and then
cocktails all round. Sensing their relative poverty, I did not really mind
treating them. I was only in Havana for a short time, I thought, and was
stunned to find that Carlos had far more in mind for me than a holiday
fling. The evening before I was due to fly back to England, he took me
for a walk along the Malecón, the seawall that runs along the coastline.
There in the hot, damp darkness, I found myself agreeing to be the wife
of a man I hardly knew.

Love or lust? Both, I suppose. I certainly wanted him quite badly.

A lot has happened in between, of course, but now here we are in Leeds and the gloss has all but vanished from our relationship. I think it would be fair to say that the honeyed words that got me into this situation are metamorphosing rapidly into something much more akin to vinegar.

"You are a mean, mean woman, you know. Always you speak about money," was the parting shot as he flounced out of the house this morning. I know where he is going and that one of my credit cards is in his expensive new leather wallet. He has the pin number and the knowledge that no one ever troubles to check the name on the card these days. Like a child in a toyshop, Carlos reaches out for everything that takes his fancy, but there the resemblance ends. He will only settle for the best quality and soon discovered whereabouts in Leeds it is to be found. New clothes were just the start. Gold jewellery, an expensive watch, the latest mobile phone...

In Cuba, he shared a beaten up Lada with an untold number of cousins. Now, a gleam in his eye, he is haunting car showrooms and I dread the day that he passes his UK driving test. Whatever he has, Carlos always wants more and sees no reason to stint himself. We are man and wife, so the profits from my little antique shop in Headingley are his also. After all, did he not leave his family and his own country for my sake? Well, he may have left them behind, but he is constantly on the telephone to Havana. He sends regular parcels of toiletries and other necessities to his Mamacita and his sisters. Fair enough, I suppose, if they are hard to find in Cuba, but some other receipts are tucked away in the drawer of his bedside table. It is hard to imagine the stringy, careworn woman I met only once before our wedding and those little girls in their skimpy cotton dresses having much use for designer perfume or silk lingerie from Harvey Nicks. For his cousin's wedding, he insists, but should I believe him? The more I nag and question him, the more he sulks and he has taken to hanging out most nights with other Cubans from the salsa clubs I took him to when he first came to Leeds. These men smirk at me in such a knowing way that I feel increasingly uncomfortable and my previous partners now give me a wide berth, so I rarely dance these days. My marriage seems to have made me a social pariah.

What should I do? If I tell Carlos that my business is in trouble and my capital nearly exhausted, he will pack his bags and leave me doubly humiliated. If I say nothing, he will continue spending and I shall have to declare myself bankrupt. I never thought that I should seek the advice of a counsellor, but I have and her words are still going round in my head.

"You must understand, Mrs Estrada, that when a man like your husband gets involved with someone like yourself, he generally sees it as a priceless opportunity to make life better for himself and his family back home."

"So you don't believe in love at first sight?" She sighed.

"Certainly I do, but cultural differences can undermine all other feelings. Why, only the other day a colleague told me about a lady who had fallen for a Masai warrior during a conservation tour of Kenya. It all ended in tears, of course, when she ran out of money and tried to persuade him to apply for a job in Tesco."

"Well, at least he'd have no difficulty reaching the top shelves." The joke was a feeble one and she leaned across to pat my hand.

"I'm sorry, my dear, but ask yourself how likely it is that Mr Estrada ever saw you as more than a means to an end?" Another pause. "I don't like to be hurtful, but I see from my notes that you'll be fifty-two next month. Do you mind if I ask you how old he is?" My cheeks were burning.

"Twenty-three."

There was no more to be said.

Well, back to the phone bill. I shall ring that number and see who answers. Then I shall take it from there. *Yo no se mañana.* Does anyone ever really know what tomorrow will bring?

Maybe not, but I'm sure of one thing. Carlos will fight tooth and nail to stay over here and he won't be short of offers.

Grandfather's Dream

Grandfather has always dreamed of crossing the sea to a better life. The result of being born in a landlocked country and such a dry one, I suppose. No one in our family had ever seen the sea before... well, more of that later.

Grandfather used to tell us that it was much easier to trade by the ocean than overland and that was why Afghanistan was so poor and undeveloped; that and all the foreign devils and career politicians in Kabul constantly sticking their noses into our affairs. He cannot read, my grandfather, but he remembers the tales he was told as a boy and used to pass them on during those long dark nights when we dared not light a fire for fear of attracting attention. Grandfather has lived through invasion and civil war, seen the main players change sides again and again to suit their own selfish purposes, and understands that it is always the ordinary people, who have asked for none of it, who suffer most.

Then came the day he spoke to Ahmad and me about entitlement. He had spent many hours talking to other elders of the village and they all agreed that the British owed us a better life. We were victims of their war. Had not their ill thought out strategies caused havoc and displaced thousands of people? Not theirs alone, of course, but everyone said that the UK was the most welcoming of all the powers involved. Once there, we should easily be able to establish ourselves and start sending money home to the family. Grandfather's beard turned white long ago and he accepted that it was too late for him to make such a journey, but he had decided to put his life savings into sending us off to follow his dream. He raised his fist to crush our widowed mother's protests.

"Am I not the head of this family, Nasima, and know what is best for everyone? Your sons will be fine. Ahmad is a man now and will take care of his brother. The fee I have paid covers first class transport, food and a safe address to go to when they arrive in London."

Our mother knew better than to argue with Grandfather, but her sad eyes followed Ahmad and me around for the whole of the time we were still at home.

"It will be all right, Zaman," said Ahmad the morning we left. Even his lips were trembling at the idea of leaving everything we knew behind us and Grandfather's eyes were moist under his bushy eyebrows. "I will look after you as I always have. Do you remember the time that crazy dog went for you and I..."

Two months later, I was fighting for my life in the Aegean Sea. Of course, a lot had happened in between. Grandfather handed over the full amount demanded by the middleman and saw us on our way in the back of an old lorry. We had left our mother sobbing at home with our little brothers and sisters, but Grandfather said she would be fine as soon as word reached the village that we had arrived safely in England.

We felt safe enough already amongst the large group of men and boys and there was quite a jubilant atmosphere at first. Then, as the temperature dropped sharply and the food started to run out, everyone realised that it was going to take several weeks just to reach the first border. We travelled on, passed from one guide to another and often on foot, until the night that shots from an Iranian border patrol scattered our companions in all directions. Ahmad was still holding me tightly by the hand as we crouched behind a pile of boulders and I whispered that I wanted to give up Grandfather's dream and go home. Ahmad said no. What else did the old man have but his pride and his hopes for us? Later on, though, huddled into our blankets, we both silently wept for our mother.

A much reduced group left the treacherous snowy mountains behind. According to our latest guide, Sharib, the companions we had lost were either dead or rotting in a hell hole of a jail in Tehran. Turkish jails were no better, so we had better trust him and keep our heads down.

It was a great day when we reached the coast and found that what we had been promised was true. The pebble beaches of Samos really were less than a mile away. There were wooded hills and a village with white houses and red roofs surrounding a little harbour. The sea was glinting in the sunlight and it was all so beautiful that I had to blink back tears of joy. Ahmad was happy too and no longer worried about being sick on the way over and humiliating himself in front of the other men.

"Samos is only an island," he reminded me, "but it is part of Greece. Once we are safely across, making our way through the rest of Europe to England will not be half as tough as what we have already been through. We are doing well, little brother."

Giddy with excitement, I started to pull off my worn out shoes, longing to dabble my feet in the clear blue sea. Sharib would not allow it. He said that we must all be patient and not draw attention to ourselves on either side of the dividing water.

"Never mind," comforted Ahmad. "There will be plenty of time to learn to swim once we are settled in England. We might even live by the sea or have our own pool one day. Grandfather knows someone whose son makes more than twenty times as much in London as he could in Kabul. You will be able to go to school while I earn enough to keep us both and still have plenty left over to send home to the family."

When darkness fell, we all squeezed into a black rubber dinghy. Before he pushed us off, Sharib handed one of the men a large knife and whispered something to him.

I asked Ahmad, "What does he need that for?"

Ahmad shrugged. "Search me! Protection from the Greek police, maybe?"

It did not seem like much protection when we saw the lights of the coastguard patrol. As a fast boat full of armed officers bore down on us, we realised that our first sea voyage was going to be even shorter than we had imagined. We put our hands up in a silent plea not to be shot and hoped that the Greeks would neither open fire nor run us down. What happened next took us all by surprise.

"Now!" yelled Sharib. The man with the knife started to slash wildly at the sides of dinghy and we all fell into the water without a life jacket between us.

I screamed to Allah for help and clutched Ahmad round the neck, but he was not a strong swimmer and I was dragging him down. Then the salty water was in my mouth and up my nose and I knew that we were both going to die without our family ever knowing what fate has befallen us. I lost my grip on my brother and kicked wildly until my head broke the surface. Trying to cough up the water, I swallowed even more. My eyes stung and I could not see Ahmad, only other men struggling nearby in the water. Then I went under again and pictured a myriad of marine creatures waiting to feast on me. Maybe it would be better to end up at the bottom of the Aegean than to wash up on a foreign beach to rot.

As I was going down for the third time, I saw the face of my lost brother, the eldest son upon whose shoulders such responsibility had been placed. Soon I would join him and Grandfather's dream would die with us. This was not at all how I imagined Paradise would be. I could not stop shivering. My throat was sore, my ribs ached and the surface I was lying on was very lumpy. But it must have been Paradise, because the sun was rising and Ahmed was looking down at me. He was smiling through the tears that flowed down his cheeks.

"It is all right, Zaman," he said. "We are safe. One of the Greeks threw us a rope and I managed to grab you before you drowned. You swallowed a lot of water, but you will be all right now."

Behind Ahmad on the pebbles stood a wet and bedraggled group of survivors, flanked by unsmiling men in uniform. No need for guns. There was no fight left in any of us and no energy to escape. Soon we would be on our way to a detention centre, but a whisper went round that conditions there were good. We would be well fed and given new clothes before they moved us over to the mainland. The Greeks just wanted us out of their country and on our way north-west.

We still have a long way to go and it is not going to be easy, but Ahmad and I will always be there for each other. One day soon we will send Grandfather a postcard from Dover to let him know that his dream is still alive.

A Deal's A Deal Isn't It?

Well, folks, Key West Airport has a very short runway, so please make sure that all bags are secure and your seat belts are fastened. The landing can feel quite rough."

Rough? Well, yes, it can be and it was. Leaning across the white knuckles of the man in the window seat, I could see how close we were to the mangroves and the aquamarine waters of the Straits of Florida as the little plane touched down. Yet the roar of the thrust reversers was one of the sweetest sounds I'd ever heard. I was was home at last.

The heat hit me like a clenched fist as I strolled across to the little collection of low rise buildings to pick up my case. Bud and his dog Mojito were waiting for me, cleaner than I'd ever seen either of them, and Bud's deeply lined face was all smiles behind the scraggly grey beard. Bud was a Key West old timer, if ever there was one, and as happy with our arrangement as I was. We'd been pen pals of a sort ever since that unfortunate incident in the Everglades and now the time had come to seal the deal.

The money I'd sent him had allowed Bud to bid an unfond farewell to the homeless shelter on Stock Island - no drugs, no booze, no pets - and to rent a small place for us in Albury Street near Charter Boat Row. I suggested a taxi, but old habits die hard and Bud insisted on walking.

"It isn't far, Miss Vivien," he crooned, "and old Bud will tote your bags." With the whole island only two miles by four, he was right of course, and Bud knew every inch of it from Mallory Square to the Hyatt Beach House and the start of the Overseas Highway. Inspired by the writings of

Jack Kerouac, the young Bud I found really hard to picture had once taken to the road in an old truck. With the start of U.S.1 only a stone's throw from the family home in Maine, he'd decided to follow it south as far as his savings would take him. When they ran out, he sold the truck and continued to follow it anyway, eventually reaching its southern end near Ernest Hemingway's old house in Whitehead Street. What happened to him over the next few decades was a rich vein of stories yet to be tapped, but he'd never had any inclination either to leave the island or to marry. That was good enough for me.

The wooden cladding of our little tin roofed house, a shack by most standards, was freshly painted in pale green and white. Palm trees stood all around it and further shade was provided by a deep porch. Gently nudging aside a sleeping tabby, Bud fished into his pocket for the front door key and gave me a gappy grin. He plucked a hibiscus flower from a handy bush and tucked it behind my ear. I blushed like the teenager I hadn't been for many a long year.

"Maybe I should carry you over the threshold?" Bud's bony frame didn't look up to the task and he gave a sigh of relief when I shook my head. The cat snorted and strutted in before us.

"Been feeding it," he explained. "Hope you don't mind cats."

"Love them," I reassured him. Key West with its roaming felines, free range cockerels and other assorted wildlife is no place for someone who only appreciates animals when they're sliced up on a dinner plate. My late husband was one such, come to think of it, with a particular aversion to reptiles. I thought of him briefly as a tiny pale green lizard scuttled across the floor.

Bud shifted from one foot to the other as I looked round. "Hope it's fancy enough for you," he muttered.

"It's fine." My first visit to the island had left me helpless with longing for one of the old Conch houses, a glorious mixture of Victorian, Bahamian and New England, but this little dwelling had also survived the worst the hurricane season had thrown at it and it would do until I wrote my bestseller. Trevor had always mocked my ambitions, but I knew that Bud understood.

We'd fallen into conversation the first night that Trevor and I went up to Mallory Square to see the sunset. The area was thronged with tourists and locals, mostly clustered round the jealously guarded pitches of the street performers. The biggest crowd had encircled a razor tongued escapologist and Trevor rushed to catch the rest of his act. Several inches shorter, I couldn't see much and wandered off on my own. Midway between the water's edge and the souvenir stalls, I tripped over a pair of skinny outstretched legs and turned back to apologise.

"That's all right, Ma'am. I hope you didn't hurt yourself?"

"No, I'm fine." I'd have moved straight on if I hadn't noticed the little dog by the old man's side. Both looked as though they could do with a good meal and I hesitated, waiting to be asked if I had any change to spare.

He stiffened. "No, Ma'am. I ain't no panhandler and I'm not gonna ask you for nothin'. Key West still got free coconuts and the trash cans are always full."

Not sure whether to take him seriously, I stammered, "I'm so sorry. I didn't mean to offend you."

He yawned. "No offence taken. The Great Rondini's performance doesn't float your boat?"

"It might, if I could see over everyone else's heads."

"Well, you can catch it another night. Sit and talk to me for a spell, if you like." I didn't really like, but I eased myself down beside him on the low wall and managed not to flinch as an aroma of stale sweat, staler beer and something I hadn't encountered since my student days met my nostrils.

"So, what do you think of our little island?"

My reply was heartfelt. "I love it. I'd up sticks and move here, if I could."

He laughed. "A lot of tourists say so and quite a few of them do just that. So why not you?"

"Because I'm a foreigner and wouldn't be allowed to stay."

"How come? Plenty do."

"Well," I sighed, "I'm neither rich nor famous and English people aren't even allowed to enter the Green Card Lottery any more. There are too many of us over here already, apparently. My only chance to stay here legally would be to marry an American citizen."

"There's your answer, then." He had turned his head to gaze at me. "A pretty lady like you shouldn't find that too hard." I smiled at the clumsy compliment, which was more than I'd had from Trevor over the last few years.

"Well, I think my husband might object for a start."

"What if he weren't around?"

"Then I'd come back to Key West and marry you," I laughed. "That is, if you're not already spoken for." I was quite unprepared for the sudden glint in the bloodshot eyes or the fervour of his handshake.

"That's a deal, then. You gotta pencil?" From somewhere in the depths of his grimy garments he produced a scrap of paper and wrote down in a surprisingly clear hand the address where he could be reached. Back at the hotel, I threw the paper away, but The Green Parrot, Key West stuck in my mind.

Over the next few days, the spell of the island grew stronger and I even suggested to Trevor that we might take a look at property.

"For what?" he retorted, hardly bothering to look up from his third helping of breakfast pancakes. "So that you can swan around pretending that you're a proper writer for the only ninety days a year that we'd be allowed to stay here? Forget it!"

I gave him the silent treatment after that, which is why he tried to make amends on the way up to Miami.

"I'll tell you what," he said, "why don't we stop off in the Everglades? We could take an airboat ride."

Recognising this as a considerable sacrifice, I was quite touched. "I'd love to, but those things are so noisy that they drive all the wild life away. Couldn't we hire some bicycles instead?"

"That's fine for you, but I haven't ridden one for forty years," he objected. "Oh, well, all right then. I suppose I'll soon pick it up again."

It was sheer bad luck, I told the inquest, that Trevor and his bike had wobbled off the path into a creek where a half submerged alligator was enjoying the warmth of the afternoon. If the sun hadn't been in my eyes when he slowed down to draw my attention to a Great Blue Heron, I'd never have collided with him like that. Everyone agreed that it was a tragedy.

So, after a decent interval, I sold up everything that Trevor and I had owned in England and now I'm going to marry Bud. He's younger than I first thought, younger than I am actually, and not bad looking under all that grey fuzz. The cleaning up process has already begun and, with some dental work, he'll be quite presentable. I've got no aversion to alcohol in sensible amounts and, who knows, a little marijuana might even help the creative process. All in all, Bud and I seem set fair to rub along quite well together, maybe even fall in love. Wouldn't it be great if our first home together became a literary shrine like the Hemingway house one day?

Fine For A Fling

Osman faced the big pile of greasy pans and smiled wryly. His life had come full circle from the little hotel back home in Turkey to this squalid Leeds basement. No, not quite full circle. Mrs Sengezer had made it painfully clear that the clientele of her smart restaurant must never see the poorly paid underlings toiling away just beneath their feet. If that had been so in Iskenderun, he would never have met Liz.

His Liz, who had arrived by bus from Adana late one afternoon. Finding no one on the desk, she poked her head round the kitchen door. Osman knew just about enough English to show her to a room overlooking the Mediterranean and he proudly refused the tip she held out. Amused, she twinkled at him. Hot and bedraggled as she was, he thought her beautiful.

He hesitated, encouraged by the way she was looking him up and down. Previous approaches by foreign tourists had removed any false modesty about his dark good looks, but none of them had caught his eye like Liz. Knowing that he would be crushed if she turned him down, he could not stop himself asking if he could do anything else for her.

"You could tell me where to eat. Not too expensive. Safe for a lady all on her own." Was that a hint that she might appreciate some company?

"Iskenderun has many fine places. Maybe I can show you? After work?"

She laughed. "All right. Why not? It's a date." A date! Now he knew that his instincts had been correct.

"Now, what should I wear, do you think?" How many times had he heard his mother ask his father that same question?

"Something pretty." Then he added boldly, "For me."

Still no rebuff, so he dipped into his meagre savings and took her to a waterfront restaurant. The waiter knew Osman and smiled at the lordly way he asked for a good table. His new lady enjoyed the prawns and shish kebab but wrinkled her nose at the Kunefe.

"First time I've had Shredded Wheat with cheese and syrup on it."

"Shredded Wheat?"

"Never mind. Wouldn't have a view like this in Leeds."

"Leeds where you live? Is it a nice place?"

"Yes. I suppose so, if you like big cities. Very busy. Lots of shops. Wine bars. Clubs. Big university."

They drank raki and watched the sun go down, then went to a small, crowded disco and drank more raki. Soon they were entwined on the dance floor and it was obvious where things were heading. Osman's first sexual encounter had been with a German tourist when he was fourteen and he knew how to please.

While Osman was working during the day, he often caught sight of Liz sunbathing or reading and could not wait to be with her again. Evenings spent in little cafés or just strolling hand in hand by the Mediterranean suited them both. So did the long nights of love-making in her room, with the windows thrown open to let in the sea breezes and the moonlight. It did not bother Osman that Liz, who generally slumbered until noon, never enquired how he was managing on so little sleep. Quite the contrary, in fact. He preened when colleagues who knew exactly what was going on praised his stamina and he even joked about Liz taking him back to England in her suitcase. She could not get enough of him, so surely something must come of it.

The morning Liz left Iskenderun, Osman told her that he loved her and took a little box from his pocket. It contained a silver ring set with turquoise stones and a note saying PLEASE REMEMBER ME. Pink cheeked, Liz said that she loved him too and fished in her bag for something to give him. He was delighted with the Leeds United key ring.

"I hope we see some matches together. You will write? Invite me to come to England, yes?"

Liz hesitated for a moment and then said brightly, 'That would be lovely.'

When no letter arrived, Osman convinced himself that Liz had lost his address and he decided to follow her to England anyway. His boss, Mr Kasapoglu, caught him painstakingly copying her address from the hotel register and pointed out in no uncertain terms that he would have no chance of getting a visa.

"We're not in the European Union yet, lad. Even if you could scrape up the fare, with no sponsor and no money to show that you can support yourself, you'd be sent packing. Better forget about it and get back to the kitchen. You're nothing special, you know. I bet that young woman forgot about you the minute she got back to England. If she'd really wanted to get in touch, she could have contacted you here, couldn't she?"

He had underestimated Osman's determination. A down payment to the local fixer and a promise to send the rest in instalments when he was settled soon had him on his way. He had turned down the 'economy' option of being dropped off near a Channel port and trying to stow away in the back of a lorry. The much more expensive 'de luxe' route guaranteed safe passage all the way to London with a heavily bribed driver.

It sounded ideal, but Osman did not discover until it was too late to change his mind that the heavily bribed driver would only pick him up

for the last leg of the journey. Nor did he know in advance that he would
be sharing cramped conditions with up to a dozen other young and not so
young men. On some days they sweltered and removed as many clothes
as decently possible. At other times, they put on everything they had and
still shivered. The food that Osman had brought for the journey was soon
gone and he had to rely on scrambling for his share of whatever the current driver threw into the back. Of Bulgaria, Croatia, Austria, Germany
and France, he saw nothing but the lonely roads where he was transferred
from one vehicle to another. One or two of the drivers were friendly,
but most were rough types who hissed at him in languages he could not
understand. At some stops, crouching fearfully behind whatever load was
in the trailer, he heard angry voices and dogs barking.

The 'heavily bribed' driver took charge of him just outside Boulogne
and dropped him off a few hours later at a safe house in the middle of a
dingy London terrace. Sleeping in a bed again, albeit a hard bunk in a
room shared with five other recent arrivals, was wonderful. So were the
shower, shave and complete change of clothes for the first time in two
weeks. The following morning he was handed an envelope containing the
English money pre-arranged by the fixer in Iskenderun and shown the
way to King's Cross railway station. Osman had never imagined so much
traffic and so many people hurrying along together. His heavy suitcase
made contact with several shins as he tried to weave his way through
them, stammering his apologies.

"Single or return to Leeds, Sir?"

"Single, please."

A few hours later, he was dragging his big suitcase up Liz's path, happily
anticipating her surprise and delight when she opened the door. Her
horrified expression cut him to the heart.

"Liz, what is wrong? You are not happy see me?"

"No! Well, yes. Just very surprised. You'd better come inside."

With the door closed against prying eyes, she told him the truth. She had gone on holiday alone to get over a painful break up and Osman's eager attentions had soothed her ego. A fling hundreds of miles away from home was one thing, but having a nineteen-year-old Turkish boyfriend living with her in Leeds was quite out of the question. She was a teacher, for heaven's sake, already applying for deputy headships, and he was only a few months older than some of her pupils.

"But I love you," he protested. "We can marry. I will be British. Start a business?"

Her expression hardened. "So that's it! No! Look, you can stay here tonight and I'll give you a lift to the station on my way to work tomorrow morning. You'll be able to get a flight home from Manchester or…"

"Not necessary. Thank you. I will go now." Osman's pride would neither allow him to plead nor to stay a moment longer in a house where he was so obviously not wanted. This stony-faced Englishwoman would never know what he had gone through in order to reach her. Aching with exhaustion and very hungry, he set off down the road without a backward glance.

His dignity intact but with precious little else to comfort him, Osman wondered what to do next. Even if he could get back to Iskenderun the way he had come, how could he return a failure and endure the humiliation of asking Mr Kasapoglu for his job back? Or dash his family's hopes? His widowed mother did the best she could with the little she had, but it was up to Osman, the eldest son, to provide for the family. Her pride and confidence in him had shone through her tears as they parted and he would not let her down. How could Liz do this to him? Her tone had suggested suspicion that he had viewed her as a means to an end, but it wasn't true and he would have done his best to make her happy.

Osman walked on and on, following signs for the centre of Leeds, until he found himself in City Square. He sank down gratefully onto a bench near the statue of the Black Prince. The Queen's Hotel was just opposite and next to that the railway station and the taxi rank from which he had set off so confidently only a short time before. Why had he wasted so much of his English money just to arrive at Liz's house in style?

He kicked out peevishly at the pigeons squabbling over the remains of a cheese sandwich. That earned him a reproachful look from an old man picking up cigarette ends and putting them into the pockets of his ragged overcoat. Osman closed his eyes to the grey sky and longed for the warm sunshine of Iskenderun. A few moments later, a blast of sour breath made him aware that the old man was leaning over him.

"You all right, son?" The bloodshot eyes were not unfriendly, but they narrowed as soon as their owner heard Osman's hesitant English. "You one of them asylum seekers?"

"Sorry?"

"Own country no good?"

Osman bristled. "Turkey is a beautiful country."

"So why are you here? You a student?"

"No."

"Got any money?"

"Not much."

"Friends in Leeds?"

"No."

"Need somewhere to sleep?" Osman nodded. "I'll take you to a place where you can get a free meal and somewhere to put your head down. They'll pray at you, but they don't ask too many questions."

"Pray?"

"You know." The old man put his hands together and gazed upwards. "To Him upstairs. Leave your case at the station, son. You don't want to look as though you've got too much. I'm Jim, by the way."

Osman reluctantly obeyed, but when he saw the forlorn queue waiting outside the church his back stiffened. This was not why he had come to England.

"No! I want to work. Find a job."

"Good luck to you then."

Osman watched his only friend shuffle inside and retraced his steps to City Square. From there, he set off to make enquiries at the back doors of the many restaurants and cafés in the city centre. His confidence ebbing with every flat rejection, he trawled the area until he could carry on no longer and trudged wearily back to the station. The waiting room looked inviting, but a man in uniform was ordering a scruffily dressed couple to leave and Osman hastily turned away.

So it was that he spent his first night in Leeds slumped in a phone box, hugging his knees to try to keep warm. Stiff and haggard, he went back to the station as soon as it was light to make himself presentable before he set off again on his quest for work. In a few places, his enquiries were met with sympathy and even a bite to eat or a cup of coffee to see him on his way. In most, he received only a blunt refusal. His second night was spent on the pavement under the Dark Arches, determined to stay awake in case anyone tried to rob him of the little money he had left. There was not much chance of sleep anyway. The rumble of trains overhead and the constant dripping of water saw to that.

In the morning, Osman counted his few remaining coins and decided that he had been going about things the wrong way. Old Jim had thought that he might be a student. There must be some Turks at the university he had passed on his way to Liz's house. They were bound to know someone who would give a fellow countryman a job without fussing about paperwork.

So it had turned out. Here he was for the time being, spending long hours in Mrs Sengezer's greasy kitchen in return for room, board and enough money to satisfy the fixer in Iskenderun and send a little home. It was a start. He was making contacts and working hard to improve his English. Once his debt was paid, Osman would work even harder to create his own bright future.

You Can Always Tell A Yorkshireman

You can always tell a Yorkshireman, but you can't tell him much! Isn't that what they say? Well, nobody could tell George Barraclough much about immigrants and plenty had tried. It was a favourite topic among his regulars at the Royal Sovereign and the argument ran along well oiled wheels.

"Coming over here and taking our jobs."

"Jobs our own people won't do."

"And sending their wages home, more like. So much for benefiting the British economy! We saw enough Poles over here during the war."

"Damned fine pilots. It was a disgrace the way we abandoned them to the Russians."

"Well, they're getting their own back now. Taking over in some areas. It's the thin end of the wedge, you know. What do you think, George?"

"Aye, well..." A wise landlord, George would never be drawn. In any case, his pub was too small and far away from the town centre to attract anyone but the locals. That didn't bother him. George only had himself to keep these days and the modest turnover was quite sufficient for his needs.

Sometimes he closed early and took a walk up to the ruins of Knaresborough Castle. He never tired of the view over the Nidd Gorge and the railway viaduct, but that was not why he went there. It was to sit on Pam's bench, the one she had requested before that final and merciful lapse into unconsciousness. The brass plaque held a simple inscription. Just her name and dates. Their memories were private, but nowhere did George feel closer to his late wife than in this spot.

Lost in his thoughts, he often lost track of time too and found himself walking home in the dark. That was how he came to stumble across a strange girl one evening in Bebra Gardens, tripping over the plastic holdall lying beside her on the grass.

The slight figure was slumped against a tree, hugging her knees and trembling in her thin clothes. A toe stuck out from one of her battered shoes.

Picking himself up, George asked, "You all right, love?" What a silly question! The poor girl was obviously far from all right, out here on her own at this time of night. Something must have happened. A row with her parents, perhaps, or maybe a boyfriend? Not that it was any of his business, but it was not in George's nature to ignore anyone who needed help, especially someone shrinking away from him like this.

"Yes. Thank you, Sir. I try sleep." Foreign too, but he could not place her accent.

"Sleep? What? Here in the Gardens?"

"Is OK?"

"No. It certainly isn't. Don't you have anywhere else to go? Family? Friends?"

"No, Sir." She looked so woebegone that George lowered himself back down onto the grass, taking care to keep his distance. One wrong move and she would bolt.

"So what are you doing here?"

"I come here for job. But not..."

Her head slumped onto her chest. To break the silence, George asked,"What kind of job?"

She hesitated and then a glimmer of hope appeared in the dark eyes. "You know something maybe? I cook good. Clean."

"Well, work like that shouldn't be too hard to find. Where are you from?" She did not reply, so George repeated the question, more slowly this time.

She gazed across as though weighing him up and said, "Krakow. I am from Krakow. In Poland."

George prided himself on being able to put two and two together. The poor girl had come all the way to Yorkshire on a promise of work and been let down. Maybe she had no money for the journey home or was just too proud to return a failure? Either way, he was sure that he could help, if only he could get her to trust him. George was a big man, but no one else had ever cringed away from him the way she had when he landed at her feet.

"I'll tell you what... What is your name, by the way?"

"Maria."

"And I'm George. George Barraclough. I'll tell you what, Maria. Take this jacket. You can stay at my pub tonight and tomorrow I'll see what I can do to help. No hanky-panky, I promise. OK?"

"Please, what is hanky-panky?"

George felt his cheeks growing hot. "I mean no strings, that is... I wouldn't expect... I mean you'll have your own room, of course." His confusion seemed to reassure the girl that he meant her no harm. At any rate, she scrambled to her feet before he had the chance to change his mind and George wondered, rather belatedly, what he had let himself in for.

Back at the Royal Sovereign, Maria gobbled up everything that George put in front of her and seemed delighted with his spare room. Later, when he passed her door on his way to bed, he heard only a gentle snore.

The sound of a shower running woke George the following morning and it took him a moment or two to remember that he had a guest. By the time he entered the kitchen, Maria, swathed in one of Pam's old aprons, had breakfast well underway and smiled modestly at his bemused expression.

"I say yesterday. I cook good." She had hard boiled some eggs and arranged them on a plate with sliced tomatoes and cucumber. As George sat down, she deftly sliced the bread and placed it before him with a dish of olives that must have come from the bar. She was certainly making herself at home but so anxious to please that she would have melted a far harder heart than George's, even though the coffee she had made nearly choked him. He could have stood his spoon up in it. Still, the sight of a pretty face first thing in the morning was something he had not seen in a very long time.

Wanting to do his best for the girl, George thumbed through the Yellow Pages and picked an employment agency at random.

"Polish, is she? And been let down, you say? Well, to be perfectly honest, Sir, there isn't much we can offer her at the moment. We've got more Eastern Europeans than we know what to do with at the moment. All well qualified and highly motivated. We might find her something in Leeds or Sheffield, but she'll have to sign up with the Home Office and apply for a National Insurance number."

Maria listened nervously as George did his best to explain. If only it were as simple as that. When he had finished, she clasped her thin hands together and said,

"I like work for you. Here. In pub."

George hesitated. It was impossible not to warm to the girl and there could be no harm in giving her a breathing space for a few days. He had to know one thing, though.

'You are over eighteen, aren't you?"

She nodded. "Twenty-two, Sir."

"All right. And please just call me George. You can do a few shifts for me, if you like. Nothing permanent, you understand. We'll see how you shape up." Not that there was anything wrong with her shape, he thought, and shook himself. At thirty-seven, he was biologically if not legally old enough to be her father.

Days turned into weeks and Maria became a favourite with George's regulars, greeting them with a cheerful smile as they walked through the door.

"Your usual, Sir?" was the first phrase she picked up. Maria said little else, but takings over the bar shot up. Having arrived at the Royal Sovereign with little more than the clothes on her back, she had stirred George's pity to such an extent that he had taken a handful of notes from the till and dropped her off in the High Street for a couple of hours. To his surprise, not only did she spend as little as possible but insisted on his taking back the rest of the money that he had given her. All the same, she was stunning in her charity shop outfits and it was wrongly assumed by everyone who saw them together that she and the landlord were an item.

While it was true that a warm mutual regard had built up between them, George Barraclough did not want any woman to share his bed out of gratitude. On the contrary, he was concerned that Maria made no effort to socialise with people her own age and put that down to a lack of confidence. No one liked to feel a chump and a few stilted phrases hadn't got them very far on holiday when he and Pam strayed away from main resort areas. As soon as he was sure that she could handle it, he left Maria to open up and went into town to ask about English classes.

George was just looking through the brochure he had been given by the library assistant on duty at the enquiry desk when a friendly voice said, "Pardon me, but I couldn't help overhearing your conversation. My name is Irena Niedzwiedzka and I am Polish too. Do you think the girl who is staying with you would like to go out with me one evening and meet some of my friends?" Delighted, George took her straight round to talk to Maria.

That was when it all went wrong. Unable to understand Irena, much less reply, Maria burst into tears and fled to her room. Embarrassed and annoyed, George saw their visitor out and went straight upstairs to confront her.

"If you're not Polish, where the heck did you come from? All this time, living under my roof and lying to me! What have you got to say for yourself?"

In between sobs, it all came out. Maria, whose real surname was Carasciuc, had been enticed away from her home in a poor Moldovan village by a fake offer of well paid hotel work in the UK. Brutal treatment had followed, the humiliation of being bought and sold and a nightmare journey with other girls similarly duped. Maria spared George the worst of it but described how she'd managed to give her minders the slip in a grim industrial estate near a railway line. With no idea where she was, she'd hidden in a derelict warehouse until darkness fell and then followed the line into the nearest town.

What a mess! The girl looked completely forlorn and George felt his anger melting away. Only one question remained.

"Why didn't you go to the police for help?" Maria shuddered.

"Bad men in Moldova hurt my family. Kill me maybe if I sent back."

With no right to remain in the UK, the girl was between a rock and a hard place. George had read about such cases in the newspapers but never expected to become involved in one. If only Maria had told him the truth at the start! But then what would he have done? Reported her? Risked his licence by employing an illegal immigrant? There was only one thing he could do now.

"I'm sorry, Maria, but I'm afraid that you can't stay here." He unlocked the little safe behind the bar and took out a wad of notes. "This will help, whatever you decide to do."

Seeing the anguish in his face, Maria could only dry her eyes and say, "Thank you. You are very kind. I go."

Maria managed not to cry when George took her to the railway station the next morning. It was too late now to tell this big, kind man that she loved him and he wouldn't believe her anyway. Why should he, when she had lied to him from the moment they met? George helped her onto the train and turned away sharply as the guard prepared to blow his whistle. Tears he thought unmanly were blurring his vision and he sprawled over one of the wooden flower tubs that lined the platform. A scream rang out.

"My God! George!" Leaving everything she owned behind her in the carriage, the future Mrs Barraclough leapt from the train as the doors were closing and was on her knees beside him.

First Christmas

Clare Markham opened her eyes and squinted in disbelief at the clock. Surely it was later than that? If the sunlight streaming in through the thin curtains were anything to go by, it must be at least mid morning and yet the house was still silent.

She had collapsed into bed well after midnight, hoping to snatch a few precious hours of rest before excited cries of, "Has Santa been yet?" began from the next room. Experience had taught her that "Not yet. Go back to sleep!" wouldn't satisfy the twins for long. Well before dawn, she and Nick would be fumbling into their dressing gowns and trudging downstairs to feign surprise over the contents of stockings they themselves had filled. Clare smiled, remembering how Nick had reassured the anxious children that the lack of chimney and mantelpiece in their new home would pose no problem to Father Christmas. In any case, however short-sighted he might be, the elderly gentleman could hardly miss their colourful stockings. Knitted by Granny Markham when Ruby and Jack were babies, they had been used every year since.

"Thank goodness we remembered to pack them," she said to the empty pillow beside her. Empty? Where on earth was Nick? A few seconds later, she also drew a blank in the twins' room. It was like one of those old films about alien invasions, she thought, when a lone human was left behind to work out what had happened to everyone else. No! That was too silly for words.

Or was it? Silence reigned downstairs too, but some torn pieces of

Christmas wrapping paper were blowing through the open back door into
the garden. Oh, no! Someone must have broken in. It had been a very
expensive year, but they had still managed to put aside enough money
to buy Ruby and Jack a few new toys. After all the upheaval they'd been
through recently, the children had to be sure of finding something under
the little tree if presents from grandparents, aunts and uncles failed to
arrive in time. Clare had agreed with Nick that they wouldn't buy anything for each other this Christmas and she had kept her promise until
she spotted him wandering red faced round Myer's lingerie department.
The last money in her purse had then gone on a snazzy set of headphones
that she was sure he would like. Now all their efforts would be for nothing, but who would have expected a break in today of all days? Surely
even the worst of criminals would want to spend Christmas morning
with their own families!

Apparently not. A sudden noise made her jump. Picking up the
nearest weapon to hand, the heavy rubber torch that Nick had placed
at the foot of the stairs for emergencies, she crept towards the kitchen
door and peered round. Clare had been determined to give her family
their usual Christmas fare with all the trimmings and evidence of the
hard work she'd put in the previous day lay all around. No wonder she'd
been so tired when she finally got to bed. Nothing appeared to have been
disturbed by the elderly woman in the bright print dress and comfortable
sandals who was standing at the work surface, her back to the door. The
burglars must have left her behind to keep guard when they took off with
their hostages. She didn't look particularly threatening, but Clare thought
she'd better play safe. Relieved to see her handbag still lying on the hall
table, she reached into it for her mobile phone and tiptoed out into the
garden to call for help.

It wasn't long before a police car pulled up at the gate and two armed officers got out. Gesturing for Clare to stay well away, they disappeared into the house. A few moments later they were outside again, helpless with laughter.

"You can go back in now, Mrs Markham. And put down that torch. There's nothing to worry about. Have a very merry Christmas." With that, they got back into their car and drove away.

"I don't understand. Who are you and what are you doing in my kitchen?"

The intruder, who was carefully arranging strawberries on top of a meringue and cream concoction, turned to her and smiled.

"Well, love, it's pretty obvious what I'm doing. As to who I am, my name is Marilyn Bromfield and I live just across the road. Bob and I got back from holiday yesterday and noticed that you'd moved in. You were fast asleep when we came round this morning. Your husband told us that you'd had a very late night and so he'd turned your bedroom clock back a couple of hours. The poor bloke was having a hard time keeping the ankle biters quiet, though, so he let them open the little presents we'd brought over for them. Then he and Bob took them to have a swim in our pool. I hope you don't mind. I offered to stay here in case you woke up and wondered what was going on."

Clare's cheeks were burning. "And I called the police on you. I'm so sorry."

"No worries, love. We all make mistakes. Now then, that's finished and I hope you'll all enjoy it. You can't beat a nice pavlova on Christmas Day. Come across and join Bob and me and some of our friends for a few drinks later on. Bring a plate, if you like. Those mince pies look good."

Clare was almost in tears. "You've been so kind already and..."

The older woman patted her arm. "That's all right, love. Don't get upset. Bob and I arrived in Brisbane as Ten Pound Poms, you know. That's what they called us in those days. That was fifty years ago and we didn't know a soul. I was so homesick that I cried solidly from Christmas Eve to Boxing Day. We just want your first Christmas in Australia to be as happy as we can help to make it for you."

Swings And Roundabouts

BURP

"Necessity makes an honest man a knave."
- *Daniel Defoe*

"That's why I've always admired pirates." Jack slurped down the last drops of cider. "They had it made, didn't they? It was a job for life. They just swigged a bottle or two of rum with Blackbeard and away they went."

"Good point," I agreed. "That reminds me, Jimbo. It's your round."

"I wish!" Jimmy tried his pockets. "Seventeen pence. What about you two? Nothing? Well, hold your glasses as if there's still something in them. They'll tell us to find somewhere else to sit if they know we've finished."

We were killing time outside the Llandoger Trow. Another group of American tourists had just arrived with a guide in a royal blue blazer and short white skirt. She stopped outside to let them line up their shots of the three gables.

I whistled. "Not bad! More legs on that than a bucket of chicken!"

"Shut up, Bill. She's old enough to be your mother. And do you have to talk about chicken? I'm starving."

"You're always starving, Jack. Try a diet of culture like these good people."

"Oh, very posh!"

The guide blanked us, but we got a few nervous smiles from the

Americans, fresh from their en suite accommodation and worried in case the three scruffs looking them up and down might turn nasty.

"Here in front of you, ladies and gentlemen, is where Daniel Defoe met Alexander Selkirk and was inspired to write *Robinson Crusoe*. The Llandoger Trow was very probably also Robert Louis Stevenson's inspiration for The Admiral Benbow in *Treasure Island*. Now we're going inside and you have forty-five minutes for your lunch."

"Have you got room for three more, Miss? We're starving!" She glanced at Jack, wrinkled her nose and almost ran inside. Her group followed, very careful not to catch his eye.

Jimmy patted his shoulder. "Nice try, mate."

Dinner at the night shelter wasn't for hours and the sandwiches they'd given us to take away that morning were just a distant memory. Jack's had disappeared before we were even out of St Paul's.

"*We* should be tour guides," I said. "I bet *we* know a lot more about Bristol than that stuck up scuttler in the blazer."

Jimmy pulled a face. "Not the kind of thing that tourists want to know. If we'd paid more attention when we *were* in blazers, we wouldn't be living like this. We should all have gone to sea, just like Mr Coombs said."

"Yes, but he meant to learn catering. Sea cooks. Not pirates."

"Well, Long John Silver managed to do both. Hey, Jack, do you remember how old Coombs made you copy out that stupid poem when you threw up in his class after you'd stuffed yourself with all those sweets? That's when he started calling you Gorging Jack."

"Well, it was the only time my old man had ever given me anything for my birthday except his belt. Anyway, Coombs called you Guzzling Jimmy because you shared them. I'm surprised you kept them down. Bigger gut, I suppose."

"Watch it! No, I just didn't have as many. Then he roped Bill in too. Sarcastic bastard! But he really wanted us to do that NVQ."

I shrugged. "Maybe we should have. Food Tech was the only subject we were any good at. I hated being called Little Billee, though. If he'd called Precious Okyjobo 'Chalkie', he'd have ended up in court."

Jack winced. "Anyone who gave Precious a nickname would have ended up in a box! Do you remember the size of his fists? He'd have made a good guide, as long as no one argued with him."

"Can you still remember how the poem went?"

"Some of it. Coombs made me write it out ten times and it stuck in my mind. Let's see...

There were three sailors in Bristol City
Who took a boat and went to sea.
But first with beef and captain's biscuit
And pickled pork they loaded she.
There was a gorging Jack and guzzling Jimmy,
And the youngest he was little Billee...

I can't remember the rest. Just as well, really. I could murder some beef and pickled pork right now."

"Well, with less than the price of a packet of scratchings between us, you're not going to get any. You'll have wait until tonight. Or go and sit by a cash point and ask for change."

"Not likely! You can get arrested for that nowadays."

I was getting irritated. "Well you think of something. How about applying to sell *The Big Issue*?"

"Did you notice all the sellers we passed on the way down here? If they flog one copy each, they'll be lucky."

"I know," said Jimmy. We could go down to Broad Quay and sit down near the tourist office. We wouldn't have to pester anyone. Like that guy

Spooner or Scooter or whatever his name was said to that BBC reporter a few years back, you're not doing any harm just sitting. If people want to give you money, they give you money. If they don't want to, they don't."

"I suppose it's worth a try. My guts are rumbling. I couldn't wait to get away from home, but sometimes I almost wish I was back. Even with *him* throwing his weight about. Mum usually managed to sneak me something when he went to sleep." Jack went very quiet for a moment.

"None of us thought it would be as bad as it has been," I said. "There's sod all chance of getting a job when you turn up looking like this and tell them where you live. 'The night shelter if I'm lucky, Sir. Castle Park if I'm not.' At the last interview I was sent to, the manager started shredding my application before I'd even left his office."

"And opened his window, probably." I ignored that, although Jimmy had a point.

"You're better off kipping in one of the subways than Castle Park. There's safety in numbers."

"That depends on who's making up the numbers, Jack. Some of the regulars go off their heads if you take their pitch. Come to that, they're mostly off their heads anyway."

"The last time I went for a job, the stuck up manageress said I should apply to Social Services for accommodation. I told her there was no point because I wasn't an asylum seeker. She said I should get rid of the chip on my shoulder."

"I wish you *had* a chip on your shoulder. A whole bag of chips. At least it would be something to eat."

"You'd have to fight me for them!"

Still grumbling, we set off down King Street. A man hurrying into a taxi outside a solicitor's office dropped his newspaper and it was a nice thick one, so Jack ran to pick it up. With no guarantee of a bed, you could never have too many newspapers to pad your behind.

"Just look at this! They're having another march against world poverty! When's it going to be our turn? They just turn their noses up at us. Do you remember all those wallies in white?"

How could we forget? Wandering around aimlessly as usual, we'd noticed a lot of people lining up and had gone over to see what was going on. A posh bloke told us to push off because we didn't present the right image for the Press. We tagged on anyway, mostly to get up his nose, but also in case there'd be any free grub going at the end. There wasn't. Everyone just stood around on College Green, holding hands to look like one of those charity wristbands and listening to speeches.

The idea came to me in a flash. "You know what? We could make some wristbands to sell and say they're for ... BURP. Bristol United Response to Poverty."

Jimmy yawned. "Never heard of it."

"That's because I've just made it up, you idiot. Don't you think it's a great idea? We'll make a fortune."

"Well, I suppose it's easier than starting our own religion."

Jack wasn't so sure. "People will think it's something to do with *the* Bristol United. If we're not careful we'll get done for fraud and end up in Horfield. I don't fancy doing a stretch."

It took more than that to put me off. "At least we'd get fed three times a day and have a roof over our heads. It didn't do Gary Glitter any harm."

The wristband idea fell through because we didn't know how to make them, but starting a charity in aid of ourselves seemed like a winner. The recycling lorry hadn't been round and we grabbed a few tins that nobody had bothered to wash and squash from a box on the pavement.

Labelling would have been a problem without John Baggs. As well as helping out at the night shelter, Baggs spent his days scrounging old computer equipment from firms that were upgrading and used it to run free training courses for the unemployed. He nearly jumped out of his sandals at the chance to help a brand new charity. Labelling our tins wasn't enough for him. He wouldn't let us go until he'd made some posters for us as well and stapled them onto an old sandwich board.

"This was left behind by one of my students who had a brief flirtation with employment," he told us with a toothy smile. "I'm sorry I can't drive you into the centre and shake a tin, lads, but I've got rather a challenging new group starting this afternoon."

We weren't sorry. Having Baggs with us would have ruined everything, although a lift would have been handy. We couldn't afford the bus and the driver wouldn't have let us get on with the sandwich board anyway, so Jimmy put it over his shoulders and we set off to walk. Unfortunately, the posters Baggs had made for us turned out to be rather too eye catching.

Soon cries of "What's BURP?" came from all sides. Life in St Paul's had been rather flat since the Carnival and people started to flock out of their hostels, B&Bs and shop doorways to join us. We could have been leading a march on the Bastille instead of Broadmead Shopping Centre.

"What are we going to do, Bill?" mouthed Jack, as we drew to a halt. Our followers, noticing a few people dropping coins into our collecting tins, were closing in on us.

"Don't ask me. There's going to be a riot if we don't get out of here."

"And it's all your fault. Damn stupid idea!"

"Thanks for the support, mate."

"I was just wondering who was in charge of this little enterprise," said a strange voice. "Could I see your permit, gentlemen? No? Well then, you'd better come along with me and bring those tins."

Our old teacher appeared as a character witness. The magistrates braced themselves for the usual excuses and yawned as Mr Coombs described us as 'honest young men at heart, despite our deprived backgrounds'. They cracked a smile, though, when he mentioned the nicknames he'd given us at school.

"I know that poem," spluttered the old chap in the middle. "It's by Thackeray, William Makepeace Thackeray. But I bet you young fellows don't know how it ends. Do you?"

We thought it best to shake our heads meekly.

"Thackeray had the right idea about sentencing young miscreants like you three." He cleared his throat and launched into the last couple of verses. They go like this:

Jerusalem and Madagascar,
And North and South Amerikee,
There's the British flag a-riding at anchor,
With Admiral Napier, K.C.B.
So when they got aboard of the Admiral's,
He hanged fat Jack and flogged Jimmee,
But as for little Bill, he made him
The Captain of a Seventy-three."

Well, they can't sentence anyone to hanging and flogging nowadays and I've no idea what a Seventy-three was! Luckily for us, that magistrate was a big show off. The round of applause he got from the court put him in a good mood and we got away with a slap on the wrist.

BURP was probably the shortest lived charity ever seen in Bristol, but it wasn't a complete waste of time. After our story appeared in the Evening Post, we were offered live-in jobs as kitchen hands. It was a start.

Fings Ain't What They Used To Be

Throwing open the shutters of his shop, Marcus saw one of his neighbours already laying out her stock.

"Morning, Julia. Have you heard the bad news? Our street's going to be dug up again tomorrow." Putting down the roll of linen she was inspecting, Julia turned to face him, shielding her eyes from the bright early morning sunshine.

"Yes, I know. I saw the notice in the market place."

"They're starting right outside my shop, you know. I'm going to have real problems with deliveries."

"And I can only imagine how my regular customers will grumble about having to pick their way through the mess to get over here."

"It's not just the regulars. The blockage will play havoc with everyone's passing trade as well. It's going to mean a fortune in lost sales, never mind what it's costing the city. You just wait. Taxes will be going up again."

"And some passing drunk is bound to fall into the hole. My husband, probably, like last time. Not that he'd be any great loss. He's still snoring his head off, the idle..." Marcus's answering frown had nothing to do with male solidarity.

"I'm more concerned about mud being trailed into my shop and someone slipping on it and..."

"Deciding to sue for compensation?"

"Precisely. It could be a field day for lawyers and people who don't watch their step."

"Or have their noses stuck up in the air, like some of the fine ladies I have to deal with. You know, Marcus, it can't be more than three months since the last time this happened. If you want a woman's opinion, which is more than my husband ever does, what's needed is some joined up thinking. The authorities could easily get together to work out a sensible maintenance schedule, but they never do." Marcus sighed.

"True enough. They don't care how much they inconvenience honest business people trying to scrape a living. And now it's the blasted sewers again!" She wrinkled her nose.

"I'm afraid so."

"In all the years we've lived here, Julia, can you remember them failing as often as they do now? I blame the clowns in charge of the city."

"I take it you didn't vote for them?" A couple of flies were determined to settle on Marcus's best loaves, still warm from the oven, and he reached over to swat them.

"I did actually, but I shan't be making that mistake again. It's their fault that the standard of work is going down and down. Forget craftsmanship! Any sensible person knows that you get what you pay for, but they're only interested in cutting costs to the bone."

"By using foreign slave labour."

"Quite. We'll have to watch out for pilfering tomorrow."

"It might be worth putting a sign up to warn them to keep their thieving hands to themselves."

"They wouldn't be able to read it. They've been brought in from all over the place, you know, and can't even understand each other, let alone us."

"If they're going to stay here, they should be made to learn our language."

"Yes, and so should our elected leaders instead of the gobbledygook they spout most of the time."

"Swanning around making pompous speeches and living off the fat of the land at our expense." Marcus gave a hollow laugh.

"Expansion, Expansion, Expansion seems to have turned into Excavation, Excavation, Excavation."

"And unemployment too. What we need is a policy of local jobs for local people."

"And proper training. My grandfather would weep at today's standards. He was a civil engineer, you know, and responsible for some of our main roads and bridges. When I was a boy, he used to take me on site occasionally. He'd explain what had to be done and even let me have a go with some of the equipment. That was fun, but I'm ashamed to say that I used to get bored with the way he droned on about his own expertise and how proud he was of his predecessors. I can hear him now." Marcus struck a pose. "He used to say, 'The way in which those men first rose to the challenges of urbanisation made us the envy of the world, young Marcus,' etc. etc."

"He had a point, though. They developed a road system, made sure we were never without clean water... and decent sewers."

"They certainly did. My grandfather said that they'd work efficiently for the next thousand years, as long as they were well maintained." Julia snorted.

"A thousand years! I'd settle for one year without them collapsing."

Marcus sighed. "I'm afraid the recent decline in standards is making us a laughing stock all over the world. My Egyptian grain supplier told me last week that there's a new joke doing the rounds at court. 'When in Rome, do as the Romans do. Don't drink the water, don't breathe the air and watch where you put your sandals down!' Cleopatra laughed like a drain and who could blame her?"

Karma

"Oh Lord Ganesh, remover of obstacles and lover of sweets, look kindly on this small offering and on our new family enterprise, which we dedicate to your honour on this your birthday," prayed Mr Patel. With trembling hands, he set down the bowl of creamy milk next to the heavy brass figure he had just placed on the shelf over the shop doorway. The elephant head of the god watched benignly as he creaked back down the stepladder and struggled to fold it up.

The September sunshine streaming in through the big window behind Mr Patel warmed his thin shoulders and reminded him of home. Just for a moment, he longed for the bright colours, the fragrance of jasmine and the tinkling of bells on a dancer's anklets. But the streets of his boyhood had also been chaotic and dirty, with few prospects for the youngest son of a poor family.

He shook himself. "No! This is home now and don't you forget it, you silly old man!"

"Who's a silly old man?" asked Ajit, resplendent in his best outfit. "Well, Grandad, you will be if you leave that milk out to go sour. If Raja doesn't get to it first, that is." He cast a wary eye at the cat. Raja would allow no one but Mr Patel to pet him. Sleek from good food and regular grooming, he was already a fixture in his basket behind the counter.

"Show some respect, boy! Have I taught you nothing? It is traditional to offer milk to Lord Ganesh on his birthday."

"Then do it in the Temple, Grandad! If you leave it there, Mum will go mad. She's been up since five o'clock getting ready for the official opening and wants everything to be perfect." Pausing only to help himself to a bar of nutty Special Barfi, he sauntered off.

His grandfather sighed. Had there not been problems enough to worry about? The shop, a former off licence, had stood empty and dilapidated for months before the Patels bought and refurbished it. Yet, only yesterday a young thug attracted by the freshly painted sign had swaggered in when he was alone behind the counter and questioned their right to do so.

"People round here want an offy, not a smelly Paki sweetshop. Why don't you fuck off back where you came from!"

"But I am not from Pakistan. I am from ..." Mr Patel had remonstrated mildly.

"What's the difference? Everyone says that we didn't win two world wars to be taken over by people like you."

Yet this foul mouthed boy and his peers must have had the great privilege of at least eleven years of free education. Had they learnt nothing in all that time about the Empire and the Commonwealth? Of the thousands of Indian troops who had laid down their lives in the British cause? Evidently not. So unlike Ajit, born in England but well aware of his roots. Ajit, who would one day inherit the medal his great-grandfather had brought back from the Boer War.

Mr Patel had managed to retain his dignity, even when the intruder deliberately knocked over a carefully arranged display. Luckily, Jagdish had chosen that moment to return from the Cash and Carry. As soon as the intruder heard the car pulling up outside the shop, he had made himself scarce, most likely to boast about the encounter to his friends. Over the hottest curry in town. A curry chosen to prove how tough they were and then washed down with cans of lager and splattered all over the road as they staggered home. Mr Patel wrinkled his nose at the thought and then smiled at the irony.

"As you would not bark back at a dog," he said to Raja, "do not waste your time arguing with foolish people. May they suffer rebirth for 8 000 years as worms in dung!" The cat opened one eye, stretched and went back to sleep.

Unfortunately, there was less and less respect these days, even within his own family, Take Hemlata, for example, when he had allowed her to bathe his cut fingers. His daughter-in-law's touch was gentle enough and he knew that she was fond of him, but his late wife would never have called him foolish to his face.

"You shouldn't have tried to pick up the glass all by yourself, Dad. You know your eyesight's not up to it these days and you won't wear your spectacles. And I still think you should have left Raja at home. Someone will complain that it's not hygienic to have a cat in the shop."

"The customers won't see him down there, so why would they complain?" Since the day that a grim faced Mr Patel had returned home from his favourite walk by the canal with a bedraggled kitten tucked up inside his coat, he and Raja had been inseparable. So many memories! The newly widowed Mr Patel had comforted his young son and then wept his own grief privately into the cat's glossy coat. He had danced round the sitting room with him on Jagdish's wedding day and again when Ajit was born.

As her father-in-law tickled Raja under the chin and was rewarded with a loud purr, Hemlata had given up and flounced off to dust the already spotless stockroom.

"Not long to go now," whispered Mr Patel, smiling with satisfaction at the thought of all the well wishers who would soon be flooding in to inspect the new shop. The trays of brightly coloured sweets in the window could not fail to draw an admiring crowd when the blinds went up. It was the finest selection in the north of England and a notice in the window was offering free samples. Only the best cashew nuts had gone into the Kaju Katri and into the milky Barfis, which were also flavoured with almonds, figs and pistachios. The flaky Sohn Papri would melt in the mouth. For customers who liked something to crunch, there was golden honey-comb textured Mesoor. Those who preferred to chew would love the Pista Halva. He also had Anjeer Barfi, Badam Barfi, Besan, Habshi Halwa...truly, something for everyone.

Mr Patel looked at his watch again. It was time for Raja to be given some fresh milk, but the first arrivals must be greeted with hospitality, not left to exchange greetings on the pavement.

He had no sooner undone the bolts and turned round the sign from CLOSED to OPEN than a scowling figure with a baseball bat loomed up in the doorway.

"You wouldn't be warned, would you, old man!"

Thoughts raced through Mr Patel's mind. Jagdish had taken Ajit with him to pick up some relations and only Hemlata was within earshot. Should he call out to her? The two of them together would be no match for the drunken lout whose beery breath was wafting towards him. Anyway, how would Mr Patel ever hold up his head again if the mother of his grandson came to harm because he was too feeble to protect her? The decision was taken out of his hands when Raja launched himself into the air.

"I hope this idiot's thick skull hasn't damaged your elephant." As the ambulance men took away the unconscious figure, one wrinkled and bandaged hand was stroking soft fur while the other reached for a cloth to wipe the blood off the trunk of the brass figure..

"Oh, Lord Ganesh," crooned Mr Patel, "You know it is bad karma to hurt a cat, so please forgive this humble creature for trying to steal my offering to you and for knocking you off your shelf onto the head of the evil doer. But bless him for his impeccable timing."

The Fat Rascal

"You won't like North Yorkshire, Dandy?" declared PC Terry Taylor. "I've heard that it's full of huntin', shootin' and fishin' types in green wellies."

"Not in Harrogate."

"Harrogate! That's a bit genteel for you, isn't it? I doubt if it's Leona's cup of tea either. Not to mention the fact that it's the wrong side of the Pennines for her. More *Emmerdale* than *Coronation Street*."

Dandy McLean sighed. A cup of tea with a fellow constable in the police canteen after their shift was one thing, but he was regretting telling Terry his plans for the forthcoming weekend.

"Och, it will be good to get out of Edinburgh for a while and I can hardly miss my own cousin's wedding, can I, especially when he's asked me to be an usher. Anyway, Hamish certainly isn't marrying into the landed gentry and I'm sure that Leona will enjoy a chance to relax and meet some more of my family before our own wedding."

Dandy was right about that.

"And a change of scenery will be good for us," concluded Leona, as the train pulled out of Waverley station.

Dandy smiled happily. His fiancée was looking particularly lovely this morning, he thought, despite the early hour. Her skin glowed and her eyes were sparkling with good humour. Gone were the casual clothes she wore to put her hard up clients at ease. In their place, she was wearing a smart red outfit and shoes with killer heels. Alongside her case, stood a brand new hat box.

"Can't wait to see you in your wedding outfit. Bet you'll look more like a film star than a social worker."

"Go on with you!" she laughed. "You think flattery will get you anywhere."

"And will it?"

"Down, boy! All good things come to he who waits."

They had to change trains in York, then it was only another half an hour on the local train to Harrogate. Hamish and his best man, Colin, both looking a little worse for wear, met them on the platform. Colin's grandmother had offered to put up Dandy and Leona for the weekend to save them the cost of an hotel. Colin looked rather embarrassed as they shook hands.

"What's up, Colin?" asked Dandy, sensing his discomfort. "Is there a problem with our staying at your Gran's?"

Hamish grinned mischievously. "Depends on what you consider a problem," he said.

Colin flashed him an irritated look. "Thing is," he explained, "I'm afraid you won't be able to share a room, engaged or not. We keep trying to drag Gran into the 21st century, but she's very old-fashioned about that kind of thing."

"Not a problem," said Leona firmly. Dandy exchanged a wry look with the other men and shrugged his shoulders.

"She's got lunch waiting for you and then you'll have time to relax before you need to change and go to the church," added Colin, clearly rather relieved. "It's only a couple of minutes' walk from Gran's house, so she'll show you the way. She's invited to the wedding too, of course. We'll drop you off and then we'll have to scoot. Last minute arrangements, you know."

Colin's grandmother had a ground floor flat in a big Victorian villa over-looking the Stray. Over lunch, she was pleased to see Dandy and Leona admiring the view and told them how fiercely the 200 acres of unenclosed grass and trees, common land for over 200 years, was protected from any kind of development.

"You two should go for a stroll," she said, "to help your food to go down."

Leona agreed. The roast beef and Yorkshire pudding, followed by apple pie and custard, had been delicious but were lying rather heavily and they still had a wedding meal to come.

"We'd love to, but we're not going to leave you with all the washing up," she said, looking pointedly at Dandy, who was quick to take the hint.

"You're very lucky," said the old lady a few minutes later, passing Dandy another plate to dry. "Your young lady is as pretty as a Yorkshire rose." It was her highest compliment, but Dandy was relieved that Leona, Manchester born and bred and proud of it, was out of earshot!

Dishes done, the young couple crossed the road to the Stray, where people of all ages were walking and picnicking. They hadn't got far, though, before Leona started to regret putting fashion before comfort.

"I'm sorry, Dandy. It was stupid of me to come out for a walk in these heels," she groaned. "We'll have to go back."

"Are those the only shoes you've brought with you, apart from the ones you're wearing for the wedding?"

"No. I brought some trainers as well and a tracksuit, just in case we wanted to go for a run tomorrow morning to clear our heads."

"Well, I'll tell you what. If you sit down there, I'll nip back to the flat to get them for you.

Leona nodded gratefully and sank down onto the only free bench. Although it wasn't in the spot she'd have chosen, being just in front of a brick built public convenience with its attendant aroma, it certainly beat standing for another minute in those shoes. She kicked them off and rubbed her sore feet. No one else was in sight, but she could hear voices through the open window of the Ladies.

"I'm so glad I managed to catch you before you left the office," said the first girl. "Poor old Chubby spent a fortune on this, you know, and I wanted you to be the first to see it."

"It's a whopper!" said her friend. "A diamond like that must have cost him everything he had."

"Well, not quite." She lowered her voice a little. "He's got contacts, you see. Anyway, I love the ring but as for the other... "

"How did you manage to get out of that without ruining the moment?"

"Easy." The tone was nonchalant. "I just waited until his back was turned. The remains of the fat rascal are under one of those trees over there." There was a hoot of laughter.

"So you got away with it! Come on, I'll help you to celebrate."

Two girls, one a slender blonde and the other plump and dark-haired, emerged just as Dandy came in sight, swinging a pair of trainers by their laces. They looked him up and down appreciatively but took no notice of Leona, whose face was transfixed with horror.

"Dandy, we've got to get the police. Not you! The local police. One of those girls has killed someone and hidden his body. I've just heard them talking about it."

"Whoah! Slow down a bit."

"Come on, or we'll lose them! I'll fill you in on the way."

"What about your shoes?"

"Oh, quick, give them to me. Grabbing the trainers from his hand, she thrust her feet into them as quickly as she could. Completely bemused, Dandy was dragged off in pursuit of the suspects. Some weekend off, he thought! The girls never turned round but headed straight for a wine bar in the Montpellier Quarter. Through the window, Dandy and Leona watched them sit down at a table and begin to study the menu. A waiter brought them a carafe and two glasses.

"Look," said Dandy, "they're obviously going to be here for quite a while. You keep an eye on them and I'll contact the police station. I'll pass on what you overheard and find out if anyone's been reported missing. But don't forget that we've got a wedding to go to."

The wine bar was busy, but Leona managed to squeeze into a corner from which she could observe the girls, although it was too far away to hear what they were saying. She ordered a coffee and took out her phone, ready to call Dandy if they showed any signs of leaving.

It wasn't long before he was back, accompanied by two uniformed constables. The whole place went silent as they approached the startled girls and said that they would like a word. A couple of minutes went by, followed by a gale of laughter.

The Harrogate PCs beckoned for Dandy and Leona to join them and the girls, far from being panic-stricken, had tears of mirth pouring down their cheeks.

When she recovered her composure, the plump brunette leaned across the table to Leona and said,

I can tell that you're not from around here. Anyone who's ever been to Bettys knows what a Fat Rascal is."

Leona was puzzled. "Betty who?"

"Not who but what," the girl informed her. It's a small chain of tea rooms. They're in York, Northallerton, Ilkley... and Harrogate, of course. There's almost always a long queue for tables, but you can buy things to take out as well."

"A Fat Rascal," added her friend, "is a special tea cake. One of their specialities. It's yummy. Full of citrus peel and fruits and decorated with almonds and cherries."

"But I still don't see..." Leona persisted.

"My fiancé, Martin Chubb, doesn't like to rush into anything," explained the brunette. "We'd been together for ages before he got round to proposing but then he was determined to make a proper job of it. He took the morning off work and went round to our house to ask Mum if he could borrow one of my rings to make sure that he got the right size."

She held up her left hand for Leona's inspection and continued, "He bought this one from a friend in the trade, then he rang to ask me to meet him at our usual place on the Stray. He thought that neither of us would have time to go for lunch afterwards, so he called into Betty's on the way to buy a couple of Fat Rascals." She rolled her eyes and added "Unfortunately, they're the last thing I need to eat on my diet, especially now with a wedding dress to choose. My friend here has promised to be my chief bridesmaid and you can see what a stick insect she is. I don't want her showing me up. That's why there's only water in this carafe and I'm waiting for a plate of rabbit food to go with it."

"I'm having the same," laughed her friend. "It would be cruel not to on this day of all days and anyway we've got to be back in the office in half an hour."

Dandy looked at his watch, concerned that he and Leona were cutting it fine to get to Hamish's wedding on time, but the tale continued.

"Well, Chubby arrived with the ring and actually got down on one knee on the grass. He proposed, I accepted and then he had a phone call from work and had to dash off. He took his own Fat Rascal with him and said that he'd eat it on the way. I didn't want to hurt his feelings, so I took a small bite of mine then waited for him to disappear before I broke the rest into pieces and scattered them under a tree for the birds to eat."

"No need for the Murder Squad, then," said Dandy to the other PCs, as Leona cringed with embarrassment. "Any chance of a lift? We've got less than an hour to change and get to my cousin's wedding."

"Do you think that we could forget any of this ever happened?" whispered Leona sheepishly as they took their seats.

"Forget what?" asked Dandy. Leona smiled and kissed his cheek.

All the same, when Colin arrived to see them off the following day, he pressed a white box into Leona's hands. It had a Bettys logo on the front, so she didn't have to try too hard to guess what it contained.

"A souvenir of a great weekend," grinned Dandy as they boarded the train. Leona couldn't help but laugh as she retorted,

"And Fat Rascals definitely won't be on the menu at our wedding!"

Vainglory

The afternoon seems to be going very well, but talk is cheap and I hope they haven't all just come for the free drinks and a chance to show off their erudition to each other. There hasn't been such a crowd of dealers and *cognoscenti* in our place for a long time; not since my father died, probably. I've done my best to keep the business going, but I know that I'll never be the dealer he was. He managed to run the inn and flog paintings at the same time, as my wife and that mother of hers never tire of telling me, but he didn't have my artistic talent. I shouldn't be vain, but I've sweated tears of blood over this painting and haven't been helped by my daughter's constant nagging.

"Why can't you *pay* someone to pose for you, Dad? I'm fed up! I hate this old frock and my arm's gone to sleep. Why do I have to hold a trombone? Girls don't play trombones. I don't want to look at that horrible old death mask any more either. It gives me the creeps. What's wrong with standing over there so that I can look out of the window and see what's going on in the market square? I'm bored stiff! All the others are playing outside and I want to have some fun too."

As if I wouldn't have preferred a professional artist's model to that lump! The way she's carrying on, the next death mask I paint may well be hers! I might have had more success in the past if I hadn't had to make do with anyone I could press into service. For this painting it was a choice between my daughter or another of those gormless working class women with their ruddy hands, strapping arms and chubby cheeks. Even Leonardo da Vinci would have been hard pressed to make that lot look soulful!

Never mind. All that hard work and irritation have certainly paid off. I thought perhaps no one would come, but the Guild has turned up in force. Getting myself elected as Headman has definitely been worth the effort, even though Catherina complained all morning about having to entertain their dreary wives in the parlour. Being pregnant yet again, which has come as a surprise to no one, has put her in a foul mood and I can hear her giving the servant hell in the kitchen. She should take it out on her priest, not me. He's the one who's always preaching that women should be fruitful, but he never comes up with any ideas for how to feed them all when you've got them.

I'm not going to worry about that today of all days. When she nagged me to convert to keep her mother happy, I only agreed to plant the seeds. They can jolly well take care of the crop. An artist can't trouble himself with such trivial matters. I'll just close the door. I've every right to preen and drink in the praise of my fellow artists as well as the rich men who might put their money where their mouth is. It's about time they took some notice of me. Some artists can churn out a couple of dozen paintings a year, but I like to take my time and give careful attention to every drop of paint. I should. It costs enough!

What wonderful things I'm hearing now and all richly deserved!

Serenity and perfection; meticulous detail; sublime representation of dimensions. Pieter de Hooch doesn't have the same luminescence and sparkle.

He won't like that. He told me in confidence a few minutes ago that he was so impressed by this new painting of mine that he wouldn't mind if people thought it was one of his. That's praise indeed from Pieter.

A fine allegory. What an intricate combination of light, colour, proportion and scale to enhance the mood and reality of the subjects.

These people really do have exquisite taste and it's very gratifying to hear the intelligent way in which they're analysing all the symbolism I've manage to weave into the picture. Two of them are debating whether my daughter is supposed to represent Fame or Clio, the Muse of History. The blue dress clinches it in favour of Clio. They're admiring the texture of the drapes as well and think the death mask is a nice touch. They've realised why she's standing in that particular spot. It's so important for the Muse of History to stand in front of the view of the Hague, the seat of the Dutch court and residence of the House of Orange. How perceptive of me to place her there!

Illusionism, technical virtuosity and atmosphere. The powerful shafts of light streaming across the canvas add a sparkle to the whole room.

That crusty old chap over there is studying the book she's holding and boasting to everyone that he's read Thucydides in the original Greek. Oh, now he's moving on to the map.

How clever to have painted a crease down the middle to symbolise the newly liberated United Netherlands on the right and the remaining occupied Spanish part, Catholic Flanders, on the left.

De Hooch is showing off again. He's just told someone that the chandelier represents the Hapsburgs and that I've left the candle holders empty to show what I think about them now that they've lost so much power and been kicked out of the Netherlands. What a clever idea!

I've noticed before how he has the imagination to transform the most mundane of female chores into images of virtue and beauty.

Too true. You wouldn't get me to do those mucky jobs, though. An artist's hands must be dedicated to his work and mine have a particularly delicate touch. The other men have realised by now, of course, that the elegant chap with his back to them is a self portrait. It took me a long time to find that costume, especially the black velvet hat, and it's coming in for a lot of positive comment.

Have you noticed how the black and white floor tiles, when used diagonally, draw the viewer's eye into the scene?

It's really happening. They think I'm wonderful!

Have you observed the way that the combination of the horizontal roof beams and strong horizontals from the map lend stability to the composition?

He's a fine one to talk about stability. The silly old man has just knocked a whole glass of wine over the death mask. I should have moved it from the table after I finished the painting. I'll slip out and call the servant to clean it up. Hold on, though. What's all that laughter coming from the parlour? My wife is in full flow.

You should have seen him in that fanciful outfit. I don't know what he thought he looked like. It wasn't cheap either and he said that the slashed effect down the back of the doublet made it the height of fashion. I don't know when, though. Certainly not nowadays. And that hat! It kept flopping over his eyes and our daughter couldn't keep a straight face. It made up a bit for having to stare at that horrible death mask he picked up in the market with that rusty old trombone. The chap he bought it from told him that it was Willem I from the tomb of the House of Orange. A likely story! He'd have been better off spending his money on a decent haircut or buying our daughter here a new dress. Did you know that she has to wear this blue one all the time? It's the only one that still fits her.

Why does he always use the same setting for his interiors? I'll tell you why. It's because he can only afford one. You can't imagine how many times we've rearranged the furniture and he still thinks no one will notice. We're up to our ears in debt and he goes and drags home that horrible old chandelier. God knows why when we can't afford any candles for it! Do you know, he can only finish two or three paintings a year. Rembrandt's twice his age and turns them out like cheeses.

My daughter chimes in: *Tell them about the map, Mother. That's the best bit.*

Catherina again: *Well, he's always telling me not to touch any of his things, but that horrible old map was years out of date. Anyway, I couldn't stand the sight of it any more, so I folded it up and stuffed it into a chest one day when he was out. Of course, it would have to be the one thing he wanted when he came home with his new paints and canvas. I told him I didn't care. I said he could tell all the other pseuds that the big crease down the middle was symbolic of something or other...*

I couldn't listen to any more. All the charm had gone out of the afternoon. The wives will pass on every word to the men upstairs as soon they get them home and I'll be a laughing stock all over town. Perhaps I'll just content myself with running the inn and selling other people's pictures in future. After this humiliation, no one will ever buy another Vermeer.

(With apologies to Johannes Vermeer whose 1665 work 'The Artist's Studio' aka 'Allegory of Painting' inspired this story)

The Legacy

I didn't expect to come away from the funeral with more than memories of Bert, but his family wouldn't let me leave without accepting a token of his and their great regard for me. Wrapped in several layers of tissue paper, it was a limited edition of a guardian angel dressed in a nurse's uniform. Bert had spotted the advertisement in one of his newspapers and asked his wife to buy it as a thank you gift for me when he left the hospital a well man again.

"Bert would still want you to have it," she said, squeezing my hand. "It represents strength, compassion and comfort. He said you gave him all of those."

So I did. Sister comes down on me like a ton of bricks when she catches me chatting to the patients and would sneer if she saw the figurine, but I suppose nobody makes an angel in a ward maid's uniform.

Bert loved to chat, although sometimes he found it hard to get his breath and could only listen. He had an oxygen machine permanently plugged in beside his bed, so that he could reach for the mask and control the flow. When he felt better, he loved to talk about his old bus routes and the regular passengers he'd had until the day he collapsed at the wheel. He'd just about recovered from that and was starting to enjoy having more time for his hobbies when the second blow fell. A smoker since the age of twelve, graduating from the occasional Woodbine to forty untipped Senior Service a day, he had to have a lung removed.

I remember when Bert first arrived in the hospital, surrounded by his family. He'd have preferred a bit of company, but Sister put him into the side ward. Patients always complain about being in there. It's very small, has no outside window and only one electric socket. That's a nuisance for me too. If anything is already plugged in, I've got to use a long extension cable for my polisher and people keep tripping over it. Anyway, Bert's family fussed over him until Sister ordered everyone out and sent me to tidy up after them. I found Bert lying in bed surrounded by presents and wrapping paper. Everything they could think of was there, from new tartan slippers to the latest *Playboy*, which one of the sons had pushed under a pillow when his mother wasn't looking.

None of them knew that Bert had smuggled in some cigarettes and matches and hidden them in the pocket of his dressing gown. Before his operation, he was up and down the corridor all day long to the patients' bathroom, where he'd stand by the window, blowing out smoke. That became our secret. I'm a smoker myself and understand how difficult it is for someone who's been smoking for fifty years to stop. Bert said that if living a bit longer meant never having another cigarette it would be a pretty poor do and he carried on until the morning they wheeled him away to the operating theatre.

When they brought him back, though, he wasn't strong enough to get up on his own. The pain must still have been awful the next day when the physios hauled him out of bed and made him sit up in a chair. Bert never complained but just gave a deep groan of relief when he was allowed to lie down again and listen to the radio. He liked comedy programmes such as *Hancock's Half Hour* and *The Navy Lark*. I used to sneak in with an extra cup of tea whenever Sister was out of the way and tell him funny stories about what was going on in the main ward. Although it hurt him to laugh, he always gave me a brave smile and patted my arm.

Everyone hoped he was going to get better. He was using the oxygen less and less, although it was always there on standby. His surgeon was due to make one final visit, accompanied by Sister, who looked up to consultants even more than she looked down on domestics. She ordered me to give the floor of Bert's room a good polish before they arrived. I didn't want to do it. Bert had drifted off to sleep again after his breakfast, but I didn't dare to disobey. I went to get the polisher and found that someone had pinched my extension cable. I hunted all over, but there was no sign of it and I was desperate by the time I got back to the side ward. Bert was still asleep, so I thought it couldn't do any harm if I used the socket for a few minutes to do the floor. If the noise penetrated his radio headphones and he woke up needing it, I could always plug the oxygen machine straight back in again.

I was ready to start when a patient in the main ward was sick and a nurse yelled for me to bring a mop and bucket and clear up the mess. By the time I got back to Bert, he was already dead. Hanging over the side of the bed, the oxygen mask in his hand, he'd been groping for the controls on the useless machine. Well, it was too late to help Bert and I couldn't afford to lose my job. I yanked his body back up against the pillows, put his mask on and plugged in the oxygen supply. When I took the polisher back to the cleaning cupboard, the extension cable was back on its hook. I never did find out who had borrowed it.

Sister said that Bert had died in his sleep from a massive heart attack. It had come out of the blue but might have been the best thing really. The surgeon agreed. The cancer had reached his other lung and it would only have been a matter of a few months at most.

Sister wasn't invited to Bert's funeral and the ham tea afterwards at the Co-op. I could only accept because it was my day off anyway. A note accompanied the figurine of the guardian angel. It thanked me for my kindness to Bert and said what a difference I'd made to his last few days. True enough, I suppose, and Bert's legacy, gazing serenely down from my mantelpiece, will make sure that I never forget it.

Not Quite Nessie

Verity could take no more of the rasping voice and four chord accompaniment to every number. It was as though the singer were conspiring with wind, drizzle and the queasiness that often follows an over generous fried breakfast to ruin her so-called pleasure cruise. Was a quiet day on the water really too much to ask for, so early in the season that the hills were just starting to burst back into life?

It had all looked so promising at first. Among the people she had noticed in the queue waiting patiently to board were a group of earnest looking students on a field trip, some middle-aged couples in hiking boots and a Catholic priest, all of whom might have been counted upon to appreciate their surroundings in a civilised manner. That was before a lanky youth with red dreadlocks had elbowed his way past them and bounded straight up the gangplank. From the moment he unzipped his guitar case with a flourish, there had been no peace but no protest either; just good old fashioned British tolerance and resignation.

Leaving the cosy saloon, Verity struggled up the steep steps to the deck and found herself an awkward perch on top of the lifeboat locker. *Koom By Yah* was barely audible from there and she could fix her gaze on the impressive ruins of Urquhart Castle in the distance instead of looking down into the choppy grey waters of the loch.

Only two other people were braving the icy wind and they made a very odd couple. The woman, so well wrapped up that it was impossible even to guess at her age, appeared to be fending off the advances of an eager young man who was wearing next to nothing. Surely the temperature on the open deck was more than enough to cool anyone's ardour, even a fetishist of the kind that Verity had read about in the Sunday newspapers. Low slung green rubber trousers were all that stood between him and death from exposure. She blinked, hoping not to witness an even worse kind of exposure. Not, she told herself, that *that* would be much to write home about on such a cold day. All the same, she thought it only polite to give the couple warning that they were no longer alone.

Hearing Verity's polite cough, the young man turned round and bounded towards her, his large bare feet splashing through the puddles on the deck. He had a weather beaten look about him and hair and eyebrows almost the colour of his ruddy cheeks.

"Did you escape before my little brother Angus passed the hat round? Be honest. He's hopeless, isn't he, but he's saving up for his gap year."

Cursing herself for lying, she replied, "No, no. I just fancied some fresh air."

"It gives you an appetite, don't you think? Would you like something to eat, Ma? The other old dear wasn't keen."

The *other* old dear? With the help of a stylist at Shear Illusions, Verity's hair showed no trace of grey. She kept herself in shape too and wore similar clothes to her students. Former students, she reminded herself sadly. It had not been easy to adjust to retirement.

The irritating young man was holding out a paper bag. "It seems a shame to let them go to waste." The stink bomb smell of egg sandwiches made her stomach heave. Hydrogen sulphide, she thought. Something to do with the breakdown of proteins in the boiling process.

"No. Thank you."

"Any minute now," he chortled, undeterred by the stiff reply and the fact that Verity had closed her eyes, "Angus will be getting out his harmonica and people will be jumping overboard to escape. Have you seen *Titanic*?" She shuddered at the thought and he added cheerfully, "I don't feel the cold, me. Look at this."

He stuck out his chest and flexed a muscular bicep. If there were any goose pimples on his person, they were probably obscured by all the tattoos, she thought, averting her eyes from the python slithering down his chest to hide beneath the green rubber.

"I suppose you have to dress up for the weather at your age, but you look a duck in that hat, if you don't mind my saying so." Verity did mind, but which was worse? This strutting idiot or his tone deaf brother downstairs. Despite the flaps of the hand embroidered bonnet given to her by a grateful Norwegian exchange student, the side pieces of her spectacles were starting to bite into the tender skin behind her ears. She could hardly feel her fingers and toes.

"You should see the colour of your nose!" he continued. "We can stand you in the bow if we hit fog. Well, I can't stand here chatting all day. Got to get the rest of my gear on. See you, Ma." As he turned to move away, she was sorely tempted to catch him off guard and push him over the rail.

A cheerful American voice close by startled her. "I'll help you to do it, if you like." With her dark hair and bright eyes, the other woman looked even younger than Verity. Round her neck were slung a camera designed for more than adding a few snaps to the family album and a pair of very businesslike binoculars.

"How did you know what I was thinking?"

"Just a hunch. Thank goodness he's gone. Did he tell you that he's planning to swim part of the way? This is his uncle's boat and he's brought all his Scuba diving gear on board."

"His uncle's boat? Well, that explains why the other brother is allowed to harass the passengers with his caterwauling. I suppose that's why you came up here? Or are you on an assignment of some kind. Noise pollution on Loch Ness would be a good topic for a feature."

The other woman laughed. "Wouldn't it just, but it's not that. You'll probably think me completely nuts, but I've always dreamed of seeing Nessie and when my marriage broke up I thought what the hell! Go for it! This is my last chance, though. I'm heading back to the States tomorrow."

"I don't think you're... nuts, but do you really believe that there is a monster in the loch?"

"Well, the water's so deep and black that anything could be hiding down there. So many people claim to have seen it and they can't all be wrong. But I've been here for a week and had no luck so far. I've spent hours every day walking up and down the shore line and this is my third boat trip. My name's Maria, by the way. Maria Tessler from New York City."

"How do you do. I'm Verity Redfearn, from Leeds, West Yorkshire." The two women solemnly shook mittens.

"And is Mr Redfearn with you?" Verity hesitated. Her private life, or current lack of it, was no one's business but her own. However, this was no reason to bridle at a friendly enquiry."

"No. We parted company some time ago. Look, Maria, it seems to have gone quiet down there, so I'm going to defrost for a while and maybe get a drink to settle my stomach. Would you like to join me?"

"I'd love to, but I'd better not. I'd kick myself if Nessie appeared while my back was turned and I missed it. I'll tell you what, though. When we get off the boat, why don't we meet up in the café near the landing stage" I've got a feeling that we may have a lot in common."

"I'd love to. See you later then."

Leaving Maria to her patient vigil, Verity made her way below. The warmth enveloped her like a blanket and she sighed with relief as she pulled off her mittens. Nothing was going to drive her out into the cold again until they docked.

Angus had left his guitar propped up against the bar and was holding court at the other end of the saloon. "I never run out of songs, me," he boasted as he drained his glass. "Just let me get my second wind and I'll give you my Bob Dylan medley. I've got my harmonica here somewhere."

Other people exchanged significant glances, but only Verity felt the red mist descend. She had read about it in court cases reported in the newspaper but always thought that it was just something invented by defence counsel as an excuse for bad behaviour. Now it was swirling all around her, thick and clammy. She gritted her teeth. Bloody Angus would *not* spoil the rest of the cruise if she had anything to do with it. Direct action was needed of a kind she had not taken since university. No one would suspect the quiet lady sipping tea on her own in the corner. She waited until the barman's back was turned to make her move.

It took quite an effort to carry the bottles of lager and the guitar up to the deck, but no one noticed. Maria was still peering hopefully into the water when Verity tiptoed past her to the other side of the boat. Forcing the bottles through the sound hole in the guitar was hard to begin with; much easier after the strings snapped. Verity took a quick look round, tossed the newly weighted instrument into the water and hugged herself with glee as it sank. She was safely back in her corner and finishing her tea when the rumpus started.

"Where's my guitar?" howled Angus, glaring accusingly at the group of students.

"That manky old thing? Well, none of us would touch it with a barge pole, but come on if you want to make something of it!"

Verity watched with interest as the two young men squared up to each other. The barman, still wondering who had left the price of two bottles of lager on his counter, shouted for back-up as the priest's remonstrations were brushed aside. It took screams of joy from the upper deck to curtail an ugly situation. Maria was jumping up and down with excitement.

"It's coming! Look! Nessie's coming! It's nearly here." The fight was forgotten in the stampede to get a good view. Sure enough, a dark shape was moving swiftly towards the boat.

"I can see two humps, but they don't look very big," said one of the students doubtfully.

"Well, maybe it's a baby. If there's any truth in the old tales, the creatures must be breeding down there."

"That's true," agreed the priest. "The stories go back centuries to the time of St Columba."

"What if its mother comes after it and turns the boat over?" asked a quavery voice. "We haven't got any life jackets."

"We might drown."

"Or get eaten."

"Then we'll sue."

"Would you say a prayer for us, Father?"

"Please move out of the way, all of you!" shrieked Maria. "Its head's coming up now and you're blocking my shot. Look at that big glassy eye and the long rubbery bit!"

"Must be an antenna of some kind."

"Don't feelers usually come in pairs? Like when we used to play Beetle."

There was another interesting range of reactions when the diver surfaced, removing his breathing tube and mask and brandishing his brother's ruined guitar. Its owner was speechless with rage, Maria was bitterly disappointed and Verity tried to look as surprised as everyone else. After a few seconds, a gale of laughter swept round the deck.

The merriment wasn't shared by Angus, who got the skipper to radio ahead for the police. Unfortunately for him, the fresh faced young constable waiting at the quayside to take everyone's statement had a hard time keeping his face straight.

"Lager louts, I expect," he choked when it was Verity's turn. "I bet that kind of thing didn't happen in your day, Madam, eh?" My day? Damn it, she could give Cher a few years... and Joanna Lumley. Still, it might be better to go along with his perception of her. Lady Bracknell to the fore!

"Certainly not, young man," she boomed. "There was far more respect for other people's possessions. Now, if you'll excuse me, my friend will be waiting for me in the café."

Nemesis

It had been a sudden impulse to bunk off Founders' Day, although we'd fantasised about it for years. Who would want to spend a July morning in full uniform in a stifling cathedral, listening to prayers for long dead worthies and a diatribe from the Head and *then* have to run the gauntlet past the comprehensive across the road? Being called grammar school tossers by Wayne Pugh and his gang was the least of it. Still, if the bus from Steve's village hadn't broken down and his mother hadn't trusted him with her car, we'd never have done it.

Memories of last year's ceremony and the day that followed were still fresh in our minds as we headed for the coast. The annual sports fiasco between the two schools was even worse than Founders' Day. It was a well known fact that the Head only kept it going because he liked awarding the prizes to the *Victor* and *Victrix Ludorum* and rubbing in the fact that *his* school still taught Latin. According to my parents, you couldn't put a price on a classical education. The school did, though, and paying the fees meant very stingy pocket money.

"And then Pugh had the nerve to dish out booze and fags to some of *our* girls behind *our* cricket pavilion! He's never short of cash."

"Well, he works in his uncle's pub, doesn't he?"

"Yes. And he snogged Natasha O'Malley-Gaunt after she told *you* to get lost." Steve just had to bring that up again!

The car park on the front was almost full when we arrived, because more than half of it had been roped off for the grey trailers of a television company. Steve parked his mother's car close by and we considered what to do. There were no girls to chat up on the beach, only a few ankle biters and their bored parents huddling in the shelter of their windbreaks. A gale was blowing in from the North Sea. This was definitely Scarborough, not the Ibiza we planned to hit after our 'A' levels next year.

"How about going up to the High Bridge?" suggested Steve. "Someone might jump."

"You'll be lucky. The Council's too worried about compensation claims." We went up there anyway. You could hardly see the bridge for all the netting flapping madly in the wind, but something was going on. At the far end, a little group stood as motionless as if Medusa had turned them all into stone. What on earth were they waiting for? We soon found out.

"Get those bloody kids of my bridge!" bellowed an angry voice. A red faced man in a baseball cap and baggy shorts with lots of pockets was stamping up and down. As we watched, a harassed looking girl with a walkie-talkie appeared at my side and gently took my arm.

"Would you be a love and move out of shot? We're having a terrible morning and the First's tearing his hair out."

"First what?"

"AD."

"Anno Domini?" She stared at me for a moment to work out if I could possibly be as stupid as that sounded.

"No, sweetie. Assistant Director. Now please. Do it for me before he goes completely off his head and I lose my job." Before we had time to think about it, we were off the bridge again and standing with a small crowd of onlookers.

"Any more *real* people? No? Background ready this time? Good. First positions everyone. Going for a take. Turn over. Action!"

The stone people burst into life and started to stroll across the bridge. Then a scooter, the rider's face hidden by the fur trimmed hood of his long green parka, shot past them, pursued by a leather clad figure on a powerful motorbike. Black hair streamed out behind him until he reached the middle of the bridge, where it blew off and landed in the netting. Bald, the rider looked old enough for his bus pass.

"Cut!" There was a flurry of activity whilst the biker had his wig fixed on again and he and the scooter rider headed back the way they'd come. The reanimated stone people ambled over to our end of the bridge and started on the drinks and biscuits laid out for them. A heavily made up girl in a very short black and white dress was looking straight at us.

"Those two aren't extras, are they?" she asked without bothering to lower her voice. "I don't remember any poncey old school uniforms being handed out this morning."

The novelty of watching the filming soon wore off. Take followed take and they never seemed to get any further.

"It must be a remake of *Quadrophenia*, someone in the crowd suggested. "You know. Mods, Rockers and all that Sixties crap."

"No, mate. It's set in the 1960s all right, but it's an episode of *The Royal*. Or maybe *Heartbeat*?" Either way, we weren't interested in something our grandparents liked to watch.

"Let's find a pub," I said. "I'm starving and I need a drink?"

"Dressed like this? We already know that we stick out like sore thumbs."

"It looks like fish and chips then and we can sit in the car to eat them. At least we'll be out of the wind."

"OK, but we'll have to have the windows open all the way home to get rid of the smell."

From there, we had a good view of the television people when they came back for their lunch and we even recognised a soap star we both quite fancied. I was all for going across and asking for her autograph, but Steve thought that would be deeply uncool.

"I'll tell you what, though, why don't we try to pick up a trophy or two to take along to the joint sports tomorrow. Pugh will be showing off with whatever he's knocked off lately and it would get right up his nose. That Rocker guy's wig would be a good one if it blows off again and we can catch it."

We followed the crew to their next location and joined a few other onlookers behind a rope barrier. A dozen shiny scooters, top heavy with banks of lamps and mirrors, were already lined up outside an old pub called The Alma when a group of 'Mods' arrived in a minibus. Soon we heard glasses clinking, laughter and a buzz of conversation, broken up every few minutes by an irate shout from a voice we recognised.

"Top up those glasses and get your cigarettes! Surely some of you extras are smokers, aren't you? No? Then we'll have to use the machine."

"Sounds like quite a party," Steve muttered enviously. "Pity *we* haven't got invitations."

"No expense spared," laughed a young woman who had just come out of the pub and must have ears like a bat. Dressed as a policewoman, she was trying desperately to hold onto her hat.

"All right, Debbie?" called a voice from inside.

"Fine. See you later." Turning to us, she confided, "I'm glad to be out of there. You can't see across the bar for smoke."

A woman standing nearby was curious. "Do you do a lot of this kind of thing?"

"Oh, every now and then. Do you know, only last week I was in a scene with..." As she wittered on, swanking about the stars she'd worked with, Steve dug me with his elbow and looked sideways at her hat.

"Looks genuine enough to fool Pugh," he mouthed.

"Don't you have to go back in for this scene?" I asked.

"Oh, don't worry, love. I'll be called if they need me. It's nice to get some fresh air."

"Well, could you fill us in a bit? Is your role very important?"

"Well, I think so. It makes a change from my normal routine, as I was just saying to this lady." Steve and I listened patiently, biding our time. Just as our expressions of rapt attention were starting to crack and we were about to give up on the idea, the pub door was flung open.

"Tea break, Debbie," shouted one of her friends and she left us. We kept an eye on her, though, and it paid off. Standing with a polystyrene cup in one hand and a Danish pastry in the other, she was at a disadvantage when a fierce gust of wind took her hat off.

"Damn! It'll be halfway to Holland by now."

"No it isn't," hissed Steve. "It's blown over that low wall and I've dumped a brick on top to hold it down. We can get it later if no one else finds it before we have to leave." Things were definitely looking up.

At last, it was all over. The stars were driven off in style and everyone else lined up along the edge of the pavement to wait for the minibus. It had just arrived and a still hatless Debbie was chatting to the driver when a big plastic box was dumped practically at our feet and a voice croaked,

"This is to go back to Unit Base. Please will someone do me a favour and take it with you on the bus?" It was the girl we'd first met on the High Bridge and it sounded as though her day hadn't improved since then. Nor was it going to. Either none of the extras heard her request or else they all ignored it and waited for someone else to oblige.

Steve and I glanced at each other. Forget the hat! The box was full of cigarette packets and bottles of beer. No words were needed. We picked it up between us and sidled off.

The following morning, we tipped off our friends that a treat was in store later on behind the cricket pavilion. Of course, Pugh found out about it and turned up too, but even he looked quite impressed.

"Bloody hell! Did you break into the Co-op?" Without giving us the chance to reply, he grabbed a bottle, knocked the top off against the wall of the pavilion and poured the contents down his throat. Almost immediately, his face turned a funny colour and his eyes started to bulge. When the retching stopped, he turned on us. "Where the hell *did* you get this stuff?"

"The Co-op at Beamish Museum, I should think," said a cool voice. Natasha O'Malley Gaunt was studying the cigarette packets. "Kensitas? Woodbines? Gold Leaf?"

She tore one of them open. It contained one very dry looking cigarette, a few flakes of tobacco and a lot of crumpled tissue paper.

Everyone delved into the box then and our humiliation was complete when Pugh kicked it over to reveal the words XTV PROPS DEPT.

"Don't you morons know that most of the stuff they use on television is fake? God only knows what they put into those bottles and the cigarette packets are older than we are."

The day could hardly have got any worse and it was almost a relief when a message summoned Steve and me to the Head's study and we found that he had company. Hat firmly back on her head, it was Debbie, although I shall always think of her as Nemesis. Well, how were we supposed to know that she was a real police officer? Oh, she gave us a thorough dressing down, but I could tell that she was trying not to laugh at our discomfort. The Director, she concluded, had been all for making the punishment fit the crime by forcing us to drink the contents of every single bottle on camera for the company's Christmas video. He would, however, settle for a written apology.

The Head was less amused to know that his school's name – so prominently displayed on the badges sewn onto our blazers by our proud mothers that it had stuck in Debbie's mind – had been brought into disrepute. Steve and I got away with it, just, but we're certainly no longer in the running for Head Boy.

An Unequal Struggle

Nightmare patterns dance across the ceiling as the first bus of the New Year passes by. Even the World Service on my new digital radio can't drown out the beating of my heart. Calm down now! Think about something else. Mind over matter. Such a thoughtful Christmas present, that radio, and much better than the usual lavender gift set. Why do people always assume that elderly ladies adore lavender? I don't particularly like the colour and the smell reminds me of our old black cat in all his glory. No free castration for pets when I was a child and my father used to threaten to do the job himself with the garden shears. Not that he ever did, of course, and pampered Tom continue to mark his territory and defend it against all comers.

I'm not going to be able to get any more sleep. How can I, when I'm only delaying the inevitable? It really isn't fair. After four decades at the chalk face and bringing up my own children as well, I think I've done my bit and deserve my retirement. I wonder if there's still a demand for chalk. Board markers seem to be the thing nowadays and teachers are advised not to use black ones if there are dyslexic pupils in the class. Is it just black on white that's the problem, or have pupils of mine in the past struggled with my use of white chalk on a blackboard? No one ever said so and it was all I had anyway. Geography teachers were the only ones with coloured chalk in those days. All those maps to colour in. Even board markers are now under threat from something called an interactive white board. I watch programmes about education sometimes, although I'm not sure why. Is it Schadenfreude or nostalgia? I certainly shouldn't like to start again. To be squeezed between the Scylla and Charybdis of ever increasing paperwork and children who know their rights.

Retirement should include the freedom to plan my day. No more bells and certainly not being pressured to abandon a warm bed for the dark, wet streets. Scurrying past the silent office blocks. Joining night shift workers and homeless people in the 24 hour supermarket. Ignoring the scornful glance of the bored girl on the CASH ONLY, TEN ITEMS OR LESS (should be 'FEWER', but the manager won't listen) checkout.

The water won't be hot yet and I really don't feel like putting on clean clothes until I've had my bath. Could I just take poor Harry's golf umbrella and nip out in my dressing gown and wellingtons? Would the few people out on the streets at this time notice or even care? Probably not, but it would be just my luck to run into a bobby. He might take one look at the dowager's hump under my pink candlewick and call for the boys with the guns. We've all got to go some time, I suppose, and that would be less humiliating than being called Ma and gently escorted home as though I've lost my marbles. All right, so I don't fit the profile, but how could he be sure? I might have been brainwashed or blackmailed into carrying a deadly backpack. Or bribed, maybe. Offered an irresistible lavender scented eternity of bliss. If I'd done more exercise and less reading and stooping over piles of exercise books, I might still be walking tall. It can't be lack of calcium. I've always loved my cheese. I'll blame it on the genes I inherited from my mother. After all, she passed on her bunions. Nothing from my father that I've ever detected. Well, just one thing, maybe, and I'm pushing that to the back of my mind. Thank goodness brother Eric was the one to get his receding hairline.

How long can I put off doing what I know I'll have to do in the end. It's not as though I'm still afraid of finding the hairy hand of a bogeyman waiting for mine on the light switch. Thank you, Eric, for making me almost more afraid of leaving my little bed at night than soaking it. Oh dear! I wish I hadn't thought of that, but if I give in now and get up then there'll be no going back. It will be light in an hour or two and too late. What was that poem that Eric and I both had to learn by heart at junior school? *In winter I get up at night and dress by yellow candle light* and then something about having to go to bed by day in summer. I must look it up some time. Yellow candle light sounds quite cosy, but I don't suppose it was. The thought makes me shudder and pull the duvet round me even more tightly. It was bad enough getting dressed on January mornings in our old house. No use praying that our mother's alarm clock wouldn't ring. It always did and only something infectious would win us time off. I used to dream sometimes about arriving at school still in my warm bed. There were no fires upstairs unless someone was ill and we often pulled our clothes on under the blankets before we got up. We must have been quite niffy, I suppose, but personal hygiene wasn't the obsession it is today. It all started when Lifebuoy invented B.O. Just imagine mouthing that at people nowadays! Still, it was one of the greatest advertising campaigns ever. Who could resist buying a bar of soap that wouldn't only perk you up in the morning for less than the price of a jar of coffee but also improve your chances of success and romance?

I wonder if the all night chemist's across the road sells Lifebuoy. Is it still open, in fact? If so, will it be full of the kind of 'loafing oafs' described by Graham Greene? Probably not. This isn't Brighton and the queue might just as well consist of anxious young fathers sent out for fresh supplies of disposable nappies. Their homes won't feature well used squares of terry towelling airing by the fire. Come to that, they probably don't have a fire. Or an airer. Does 'all night' mean a twenty-four hour service like the supermarkets? Except on Sundays, of course. It's a long time since all the alcohol had to be covered up outside licensing hours, but the Sunday trading laws seem to be here to stay. Not that there's much you can't find on sale at petrol stations these days. Milk, flowers, newspapers, cigarettes... It's a wonder they still find room for the pumps. Anyway, I doubt if either the chemist's or the petrol station will have what I need. It will have to be the long walk to the supermarket. No time for dalliance by the freezers or thumbing through the magazines by the coffee machine this morning, though. Straight in and out and home.

At least it isn't icy at the moment. If it were, coming back down the hill would either take me ten minutes or ten seconds, with nothing in between. No more trips to Casualty, thank you very much! Having my dislocated shoulder sorted out last winter was the closest I've come to medieval torture. No morphine either. The doctor told the nurse who suggested it that the patient needed to *feel* when the joint went back in and I certainly did. Too much to object to his use of the third person and lofty indifference to my agony. On the other hand, it jarred when the little nurse asked me gently if 'we' were feeling any better.

Why is the darkest hour supposed to be just before dawn? Is it just a saying, or is it true that we're at our most vulnerable then? Something to do with blood pressure going up as we gird our loins to face whatever the day is going to throw at us. How often have I lain awake in a cold sweat at three or four o'clock in the morning and felt my heart racing? Wondered who would sort out all my affairs and what kind of a turn out there would be at the funeral. I suppose it would depend on the weather and what was offered afterwards by way of refreshments. A cold, wet day in winter and a few plates of sandwiches would hardly entice crowds of mourners to my graveside. Gone are the days when even the lure of a ham tea at the Co-op could fill the pews. Anyway, where exactly are our loins and how do we gird them? Not with the kind of girdles most women wore until the

1960s. Foundation wear giving them nipped in waists and chests lifted to just below their chins. That style wouldn't have suited Odysseus or Thor or even the Lady of Shallott, all famous girdle wearers. Some kind of belt, then, occasionally with magical powers.

In the shadows, there's a stirring that would terrify a believer in magic. A dark form is writhing towards me. Should I ignore him? I could. I really could, even now when he's breathing right into my face and his menacing rumble is making the bed shake. If I open my eyes, I know that I'll see that uncanny glow. 'The Devil's fire' they called it in the Middle Ages, when his kind was persecuted. It's lucky that I'm not superstitious. A battle of wills is beginning that I know I'm going to lose. A little gentle pressure on my throat and he's won. I stare into triumphant green eyes. We both know what my father passed down to me. A healthy dose of ailurophilia. There's a word to conjure with at this hour of the morning and one not included in every dictionary. Combine the Greek words 'ailuros' meaning 'cat' and 'philos' meaning 'fond of' and you end up with an old softie about to sacrifice a comfortable lie in for the sake of Tom VII. After all, it isn't his fault that supplies ran out last night.

All right! I'm getting up now and going out to buy some blasted cat food!

Money Well Spent

After James died, I thought food might be the answer and hit the Häagen Daz with a vengeance. My smart London friends are convinced that I'm having an early mid-life crisis, sparked off in all probability by catching sight of myself in the mirror. They're all telling each other, in the strictest confidence, of course, that poor Kate is in despair over the weight she's put on since her sad loss. It's quite acceptable for grieving widows to fade away, but not to expand to a wobbly size... Well, never mind what size that is!

The latest recruits to the chorus of disapproval are my parents-in-law, although they were very supportive while they still saw a gleam of hope in my rapidly expanding waistline. How ironic that would have been! A mini-James on the way. A posthumous heir for a son who swore to his parents that he'd love to start a family but made very sure that his wife didn't forget to take her pills. A husband who sent extravagant presents to his two odious nieces but browbeat his wife with his insistence that children of our own would ruin his hard won life style. The same life style that killed him before he reached forty.

Now, of course, it's all about James's money. Well, it's my money now and they hate that. I'd love to be a fly on the wall when they realise that I've actually gone. Out of their reach to spend the summer with someone they've never met. Someone I've never actually met either. A tall, slender, dark and very young someone. I'm safely on the coach now, my phone's switched off and anyway it's far too late for any of them to talk me out of my decision.

I wonder if I should wave to that woman teetering on the kerb. I know she's seen me. Arabella something. James's childhood sweetheart. She made a spectacle of herself at our wedding. Too much champagne followed by sobbing into the strawberries. No cream, of course. Her legs are so thin that they'll snap if she falls over. She's brandishing some shiny carrier bags. Fine. I can respond with my passport and guidebook. She's been buying more Manolos, I expect, or size 6 designer outfits. It was a real pleasure to send all mine to a charity auction, to be fought over by stick insects like her. Women who are still pretending to enjoy an early morning jog with their personal trainers. Followed by a breakfast of hot water and lemon. I'll have a late breakfast at Heathrow. There should be plenty of time before the flight. Let me think. Shall I have the Continental or the full English? Oh, I'll decide when I get there. Full English, probably. It will be the last chance for a while. Arabella is clutching her phone now. One guess whose number she's tapping in and what they're going to say about me. We're moving off now, but I could write the script.

"I'm sure it was your sister-in-law in the airport coach. She saw me looking and held something up at the window. She looked very pleased with herself."

"Pleased with herself? So she's actually going through with it. I never thought she'd have the confidence for such a long journey on her own. She never went further than Knightsbridge without James, you know. Once the novelty value wore off, her clinginess bored him to tears, especially at parties when he needed to circulate, to work the room. He gave her carte blanche to spend what she liked and then she had the gall to say that swiping his gold card was the closest she got to him some weeks. She never showed any gratitude, not even to our parents for the wonderful wedding they insisted

on paying for because she had no family of her own to do the honours. Do you remember how much effort they put into it?"

"Of course I do. Champagne and roses all the way. And, as they drove away in that vintage Rolls, your mother said that they looked so happy that we'd soon be hearing the patter of tiny feet."

"Yes, well, Kate couldn't even get that right. James told us that she wasn't interested in having a family. She wouldn't have got involved with that foreign boy if she'd had children to look after."

"Remind me. How did she get involved with him?"

"Oh, through the Internet, apparently. She's been very cagey about it, but I think it's been going on for a long time."

"While poor James was still alive, do you mean? How ghastly! I mean, I know your brother was no angel. These City boys never are. Too many pretty girls in the office. But he always came back to her. Took her to Cannes, St. Moritz, the Bahamas..."

"She once said to me that the only way to get his attention in between holidays was to wrap herself in a balance sheet and lie down on his desk. If she could get past his secretary. Not a word of gratitude for all the lovely things he bought for her and for their home. She just took it all for granted. She's very selfish, you know. Not only refused to have children of her own, even though Justin said that they could afford a place in the country as well as the Chelsea flat, but she shows absolutely no interest in my girls. Chloë desperately needs a new pony and I've been dropping hints about the outrageous rise in their school fees. Madam just smiles sweetly and changes the subject. I wish that James had married you, Bella. You'd have suited him much better and maybe he'd still have been alive."

"You know how much I wanted to marry him. James had... was... everything I'd ever hoped for. But what about Kate's new chap? What does he have going for him?"

"Nothing much, as far as I can gather. No money, anyway. She told me that she fell for him the moment she saw his photograph."

"Sounds like a con job to me."

"That's what I said, but Kate wouldn't listen. She said that all the information checked out and she'd made up her mind to go over there and meet him in the flesh, so to speak." There was a pause, while both women wrinkled their noses.

"A lot of women with more money than sense have been taken in like that," continues Arabella eventually. "Do you remember Tamara Lytton-Jones hooking up with that young sailing instructor she met in Mauritius? She spent a fortune on him, paid for him to come over here..."

"Yes, I know. He stayed until he'd drained her dry and then disappeared. Well, Kate's told us that there's no question of that with her Khushal."

"So that's his name, is it? Do you think she might be planning to move in with him permanently over there?"

"I doubt it, although I know she's been sending money across. She's very touchy, though, and I don't want us to fall out. If it all comes to grief, which I sincerely hope that it will, she might be more amenable to doing something for Amelia and Chloë. It's what James would have wanted. He was always very generous towards them, you know."

"Of course he was. Poor James. He must be rolling in his grave over all this!"

Well, there's no turning back now and it's a good omen that my flight is leaving on time. The sun's beating through the window and people are already complaining that it's too warm in the cabin. I'm glad that I decided to travel in a cotton frock and comfortable sandals, my hair scraped back off my face. No one would recognise the trophy wife James used to wheel out to impress his friends or the senior partner. The trophy wife

who wore a new outfit for every charity ball, gallery opening, première...
But Khushal won't judge me by my clothes. Making contact with him
has been the best thing I've done since we had to move south to further
James's career.

I was a trim size 10 then and he was happy with that, until he met
all those City girls in their sharp suits. We'd hardly unpacked before he
started to buy me snappy little tailored numbers to smarten me up and
taking me to the sort of restaurant where the main course is the size of
an amuse-gueule. I joked once that it didn't amuse this girl and one of the
partners' wives actually took it upon herself to give me a French lesson
on the spot. James thanked her and looked daggers across the table in
case I told her to keep her own *gueule* shut.

I still had spirit in those days, but it wasn't long before I resigned
myself to a fashionable existence in ever tighter, smarter and more expensive clothes that left no room for decent helpings, much less seconds. Life
with James was one continual upgrade and, if he hadn't died, I'd probably
have reached size zero. Any hint of strain on my child sized waistbands
and I was booking myself in for more circuit training or an extra Pilates
class. James, meanwhile, was working a sixteen hour day and then dash-
ing off to play squash or to join other boozed up City boys in whichever
bar was currently in favour.

Khushal wrote me a quaintly expressed but very sympathetic letter
when Justin died. I didn't think he'd ever have heard of squash, but
apparently it's hugely popular in India. He's read a lot about it, although
he's never had the chance to play. It's an excellent game, of course, if you
practise regularly with a partner of similar ability. Not so good if you're too
obstinate to accept that the young whippersnapper who's just joined the
firm can run rings round you. Even worse, if you're hopelessly outclassed
but insist on carrying on until you collapse. The young whippersnapper

sent me flowers and apologies, but it wasn't his fault. James never did know when enough was enough.

Khushal's letters are such a big part of my life that I've brought the latest one with me to read again during the flight. He's enclosed a photo, so that I can see him wearing the shirt I sent for his last birthday. It really suits him. He's smiling into the camera and it feels as though he's looking straight at me. I wish I could ruffle his dark hair. It's far too neat. He's sent a poem too and another little sketch of his village. There's so much it lacks, but I know how fond he is of it and of all the people who live there. Most seem to be related to him one way or another and he writes in such detail that I feel I know them already.

I'm not going to get much conversation out of the man in the next seat. The faint noise coming out of his headphones won't disturb me. I've got plenty to think about. Number one on the list is my sister-in-law. James's parents have more or less cut me off, but she's always on the phone. What was the last thing? Oh, yes. Amelia has been invited to spend a couple of weeks in Courchevel but really needs new skis. Fat chance! She can get herself a job as a chalet maid and buy her own. She and Chloë have always been spoilt brats and their mother's comments on my plans to spend the summer with Khushal were downright vicious.

The flight's passing quickly and the lunch I've been served wasn't bad at all. The old Kate would just have messed it about with a fork and filled her stomach with sparkling water. The new Kate has eaten it all and washed it down with a couple of glasses of Sauvignon Blanc. Time for a doze and then I'll get out my guidebook again. It's nearly falling to pieces now, but there's still plenty more to learn about Khushal's part of India.

I'm starting to regret the fact that my uncommunicative neighbour left the plane in Qatar. This young American who's taken his place is friendly but far too earnest. Before the seatbelt sign went off, he'd told me all about himself. He's called Kenneth Gershen and he's from Long Beach, California. He's just finished his medical studies and is now on his way to take up a voluntary placement in a hospital in Hyderabad. Does he ever pause to take a breath?

"It's not enough, you know, Ma'am. The West should be doing far more to help. Poor families can't afford to travel miles from their homes to the city. There should be a medical centre in every area, a basic clinic in every village. Health visitors. Many of the children are thin and sickly."

He's right, of course. I know more about rural poverty in Andra Pradesh than he'd give me credit for. In his stilted English, Khushal has explained how hard it is for people to scrape a living and see even the most modest of their dreams come true. The new pump is a constant source of delight to the women who no longer have to trudge down to the river several times a day in the blazing sun. Khushal's grandfather thinks that this will make them slothful and forget their place, but he doesn't agree. They know that clean water will stop their babies becoming ill. Babies. The only thing, apart from his time, that James was never willing to give me. They just weren't part of his game plan. I'm sure that Khushal doesn't think like that. He writes so expressively about the jolly pranks the children in his village get up to. Jolly pranks! His vocabulary is straight out of 1940s adventure stories for boys.

Ken has noticed me smiling and looks reproachful. "Tourists," he began, the 'like you' silent but obvious, "have no idea. They think that visiting the Taj Mahal and going for an elephant ride is somehow going to do wonders for the local economy." He glares at my guidebook as though he'd like to rip it to shreds. "What the Indian people need are income generating schemes, seeds, tools and livestock. Children are dying every day from contaminated water and malnutrition and no one cares. Tourists stay in smart hotels and pay a few rupees to take a photograph of a picturesque beggar. Where are you staying, by the way? The Taj Residency? Five star comfort and room service?"

How dare this angry young man judge me! "I'm staying with an Indian friend, actually. We met on the Internet." That's stopped him in his tracks. One look at Khushal's photograph and then back at me and he's got nothing else to say. I wonder if he's heard of Tamara Lytton-Jones and her sailing instructor.

Rajiv Gandhi International Airport is noisy and chaotic and it's taking a long time to get through Immigration. Then I have to wait for my cases, but I don't mind. I'm picturing the look on Khushal's face when he sees the surprise presents I've brought him. Unlike my sister-in-law and her brood, he never asks for anything for himself.

Walking through the final barrier, I've never been more nervous in my life. What if Khushal doesn't recognise me from my latest photograph? What if he hasn't been able to get here at all?

I needn't have worried. Here he comes now, elbowing his way through the crowd in International Arrivals. It looks as though half the village is following on behind, all waving and smiling. They must have clubbed together to hire a bus.

"Auntie Kate! Auntie Kate!" He doesn't throw himself into my waiting arms as an English boy might have done. Instead, he kneels to touch my feet. A lady is coming forward shyly, her head bowed, to greet me. She presses her hands together and holds them near her heart.

"*Namaste.*" I follow her example and we smile at each other. Khushal's mother is probably younger than I am, but the black bindhi on her forehead shows that she too is a widow.

His thin shoulders bowing under the weight of my luggage, the boy

I'm sponsoring through secondary school and whose whole community I'll continue to help as much as I can leads the way out of the airport.

Crabtree Manor

I'd have given anything to live in a big mock Tudor house like Crabtree Manor, although the Crabtree family took it all for granted.

Peeping through their front door as a child, the first thing I saw was an impressive hall. It had a black and white tiled floor and separate stands for the Crabtrees' coats and umbrellas. There was a small round table with twisted legs for their telephone as well. That was in the days before everyone had a telephone and several years before my family could afford one. If we needed to ring someone, we made sure that we had the right change and then walked to the phone box several streets away.

To the right of the hall was a luxuriously furnished sitting room with a three piece suite and a television and to the left a dining room. Beyond that was the kitchen, equipped with a big fridge – no sour milk in the summer for the Crabtrees – electric cooker and every modern labour saving device. My mother still had to do all our laundry by hand, but Mrs Crabtree had an automatic washing machine *and* a maid to operate it.

Upstairs was just as grand. The parents had beautifully polished bedroom furniture, including an imposing four poster with blue brocade curtains. The children, Charlotte and Cedric, had nursery rhyme wallpaper, a neat little bed each, their own wardrobe and chest of drawers and a wooden box overflowing with toys. Their Scottie dog was usually up there too. Unlike my mother, Mrs Crabtree didn't consider it unhygienic to let an animal sleep on your bed. The maid's room was under the eaves and much more plainly furnished than the others but still very comfortable. She had her own washstand with a big china jug and bowl set more suitable for a Victorian house than mock Tudor. That was because she wasn't allowed to use the family's bathroom.

Not for the lucky Crabtrees a chilly walk to an outside lavatory first thing in the morning, followed by a quick wash in the kitchen sink, which was all I knew in those days. No wonder they kept their luxurious facilities to themselves! They could soak every day if they wanted to in their big bath, step out onto a fluffy carpet and choose from the neat piles of matching towels. I'd never seen anything like it before, except at the cinema.

The cost of electricity meant nothing to the Crabtrees. The curtains in their house were rarely drawn and light shone through the diamond panes of every window. They didn't really seem to appreciate any of their fine things, though. During all the years we were close neighbours, their expressions never changed. All my family ever got from any of them was a haughty stare, even when my father worked until all hours redecorating their home or my mother sewed until her fingers were sore to reupholster their three piece suite and make matching curtains.

One day, I decided to put the wind up Mrs Crabtree by putting Snowy through her front door, but I still got no reaction. She didn't scream or climb onto a chair when he scampered straight past her and up the stairs. She just ignored him. Only my father was cross when he found out and said that I should have known better. That house had cost more money than I could ever imagine to build and furnish and not even a sour bunch like the Crabtrees deserved to have mouse droppings all over the place. I was made to apologise and clean up the mess.

My attitude to the Crabtrees hardened even further after that, but when I finally found myself in a position to evict them, the buyer of their house took pity and decided to keep them on as tenants.

Looking back on it, I regret the transaction. I should have kept

Crabtree Manor to pass on to my children. Only my father, who had painstakingly built the place from scratch on the kitchen table, objected at the time, but he let me have my own way. After all, what new teenager in the 1960s wouldn't part with a doll's house in order to raise the funds to buy a record player?

He Who Laughs Last

Writers' circles are made or broken by the give and take between members and Frank's obsession with William Makepeace Thackeray is putting ours under severe strain.

A self styled expert, Frank can find a way of introducing his idol into every theme we choose and he loves to draw parallels between their lives. Thackeray was born in India. Frank comes from Manchester but had Indian neighbours. They were both miserable at school, poor at sport and – Frank always taps his prominent, misshapen nose at this point – came off badly in fights. We must consider their shared love of reading novels and sketching, or their coming second in poetry competitions. Thackeray lost to a fellow student called Alfred Lord Tennyson; Frank to Adrian Henry. They both dropped out of university and travelled on the Continent. Thackeray associated with a bad crowd, had a bout of syphilis and accumulated large gambling debts. Frank hitchhiked across Europe, had a broken leg set in München-Gladbach and accumulated large blisters. He hints at unsavoury encounters but will never be more specific. Later on in life, they both dabbled at a variety of jobs and their marriages turned out badly. Isabella Thackeray fell victim to mental illness and spent most of her life in an institution. Frank's wife Marjorie spends most of *her* time watching the shopping channels on Sky and avoiding Frank.

This releases him to spend six evenings a week at his desk trying to emulate Thackeray's style and the seventh in the back room of The Sun in Splendour sharing the results with us. He listens impatiently as we read out our latest work, stifling a yawn or tapping his knee if anyone goes on too long. Brenda dreams of creating a second Mr Darcy; third, if you count the one in *Bridget Jones*. Shirley focuses on environmental issues and Marianne is a poet. Stephen's pieces regularly appear in fishing or gardening magazines, Bill writes about furniture restoration and the supernatural and Edward is writing a comedy about his experiences in the Royal Navy. As for myself, I write about anything and everything, see my work in print occasionally and have a large stack of rejections to brood over.

Once a year, we set off to cover some literary geography. We've walked in the footsteps of the Brontës in Haworth, Dickens in Broadstairs, Alan Bennett in Leeds and William Cobbett in Farnham. On that occasion, Shirley persuaded us to hire bicycles and follow the path of one of the '*Rural Rides*' that Cobbett took on horseback. Never again!

This year, Frank was determined that it should be a tour of Thackeray's old London haunts. He dreamed of walking along Pall Mall and through the enormous front door of the Reform Club. Did we have any contacts who might give us access to the Guest Room to see Thomas Lawrence's famous portrait of the great man? Sadly, no one had, but Frank was undaunted. A superb way to finish our Thackeray day would be to drive on to Tunbridge Wells and have dinner in his old home, Rock Villa, now the location of a very upmarket restaurant.

Only Brenda vehemently opposed Frank's plans. For years, she had suggested Bath and been disappointed. The prospect of a day devoted to a genteel woman writer obsessed with balls and parlour based quests for suitable spouses had never appealed to the men in the group. Once again, poor Brenda spread out her brochures and tried to convince them that there was a lot more to see in Bath than the Jane Austen Centre in Gay Street. They snorted and she knew that she was wasting her breath.

So, London and Tunbridge Wells it was to be. Brenda refused the drink offered by Frank to show that there were no hard feelings, gathered up her brochures and left tight lipped.

Frank insisted on driving the minibus we hired for the outing. He had demanded an early start, so we were yawning outside The Sun in Splendour before six o'clock. He drew up and waited impatiently for us to take our places behind him. A pile of guidebooks and maps on the seat beside him discouraged any would be navigators. It was still dark and the conversation, lively at first, petered out as people started to doze off.

We were awoken by the sudden silence as Frank switched off the engine. The dawn light showed a motorway as straight as the Roman road beneath it and lines of stationary vehicles stretching out as far as we could see.

A chirpy driver leaned out of his cab. "Hope you're not in any hurry, mate. There's been a big pile up. It's going to take hours to shift." Frank reddened, but he wasn't going to be beaten. He consulted one of his maps and announced triumphantly,

"I know how to get us out of this. We're not far from the next junction and from there we can get over to the A3. We'll be in London in no time if I put my foot down!"

We braced ourselves. People hooted as we passed them on the hard shoulder to get to the slip road, but there were no police cars in sight and drivers behind us followed Frank's example. Followed by a long procession, we were soon bumping along a road so minor as to be unworthy of the name. Unfortunately, just as we passed a sign for Alton, a similar convoy appeared in the distance, heading towards us.

"I shouldn't go that way, pal. The A3's blocked. Why don't you turn round and follow us to the motorway?" Disappointed, we watched Frank pull into a lay by to study his maps again. Only Brenda looked pleased, but it was more than Schadenfreude. Her face was flushed and she was bursting with suppressed excitement.

"Do you all know where we are?" Wordlessly, we turned back to look at the Alton sign. "Yes, I know, but we're only a couple of miles from Chawton."

"So?"

"Well, who lived in Chawton? Jane Austen, that's who!"

For once, Frank was thwarted. It was already getting on for lunchtime and only *he* thought that there was still a realistic chance of getting to London in time for the visit to be worthwhile. He grudgingly drove us to Chawton but refused to get out of the minibus when we arrived at the pleasant red brick seventeenth century house where Jane spent the last few years of her life.

There really was something for everyone. Brenda, still pink with pleasure and with a proprietorial air, took great delight in pointing out the small round table upon which Mr Darcy was created. Shirley, Marianne and I enjoyed poring over examples of Jane's jewellery and needlework, especially the patchwork quilt she made with Mrs Austen and Cassandra. Bill gazed covetously at the Reverend Austen's Hepplewhite chairs and bureau-bookcase with its precious first editions. Edward was thrilled to find memorabilia of the two of Jane's brothers to have distinguished naval careers. Stephen enjoyed the peace of the garden with its array of old varieties of flowers and herbs.

It was only later, when we had seen all there was to see and had a group photograph taken around Jane's donkey carriage in the old bake-house, that we walked back to where we had left Frank and the minibus and found that both had disappeared. His mobile was switched off too. Agreeing with Edward that the 'blighter' had gone off in a huff, we decided that there was nothing for it but to leave a message for Frank and walk into the village to find some refreshments. At least it would be a good opportunity to get out our notebooks and record some impressions of the day.

After a couple of hours, that was wearing very thin, even though Brenda passed round some of the books she'd bought from the little shop at the Austen house. There's a limit to how many cups of coffee and slices of cake marooned writers can face and Bill was just enquiring about transport to the nearest railway station when we saw the minibus heading towards us. It should have been sharpened pencils at dawn, but Frank's beatific smile disarmed us. As relaxed and cheerful as I've ever seen him, he chuckled,

"You'll never guess where I've been! I was heading for Northington to try to find The Grange where Thackeray stayed with the Barings, but somehow I ended up in Winchester. It must have been fate, because *Vanity Fair* was on at the cinema. It's a wonderful film and you'll never guess what, Brenda! The couple sitting next to me said that the London scenes weren't shot in London at all. They were done in and around Great Pulteney Street in Bath. So, if you want to go there next year, you'll have my vote."

Laughing heartily, he ushered us into the bus and off we went.

About The Author

Born in Leeds, Maggie Cobbett ventured across the Pennines to study at the University of Manchester and then spent more years than she cares to remember teaching French, German and EFL in the UK and abroad. Now settled with her family and two ex-feral cats on the edge of the Yorkshire Dales, Maggie takes inspiration for her writing from her surroundings, travels, family history and her work as a television background artist.

Visit Maggie online at http://www.maggiecobbett.com

About The Stories

'Murder in the Second Act' and 'The Fat Rascal' originally appeared in The Weekly News as part of the 'The New Adventures of Dandy McLean' series, to which Maggie was a regular contributor.

'Too Much Blood on the Axminster' was the winning entry in a competition run in conjunction with the 2011 Theakston's Old Peculier Crime Writing Festival.

'Plenty More Where She Came From' was first published in Writers' News, having won first prize in its short story competition.

An earlier version of 'Fine For A Fling', entitled 'Not Wanted', is included in 'Migration Stories', a Crocus book launched by Commonword in 2009.

'Fings Ain't What They Used To Be' was first published in The Weekly News.

An earlier version of 'Karma' was written for the 2008 Cats Protection Writing Competition and appeared in a special competition supplement.

Printed in Great Britain
by Amazon.co.uk, Ltd.,
Marston Gate.